He didn't know why his face was buried in long strands of sweet-smelling hair.

A bird squawked in the background and it rattled Rafe all the more when a woman shifted out from under him, sat up and forced him to do the same. What were they doing on the ground? *Dr. Robinson. God, had he attacked her?*

"Are you okay?" she murmured. "You had a small flashback and fell over a feed bucket. It was my fault. I saw the bucket, but didn't move it out of the aisle. I swear I'll be more careful in the future."

Her cool, seductive touch telegraphed a signal to Rafe's body. Even though he couldn't see the woman who hovered so close to him, he was still a man. All man.

Dear Reader,

My extended family is a great, eclectic mix of teachers, cops—including bike and horse patrol—retail people, kids from elementary school to college, and retired and current military. It makes for interesting, lively conversations and endless stories at our family gatherings.

We're also big supporters of political causes from animal rights to the homeless and nearly all veterans groups. Men and women go to war to protect home and family. Some don't return. Some come back injured. Doctors and love help put the shattered back together. That's what Dr. Alexa Robinson and Major Rafe Eaglefeather's story is all about. Family, love and healing. I hope you'll come to care for them as I have.

Sincerely,

Roz Denny Fox

P.S. As always, I love to hear from readers. E-mail me at rdfox@cox.net, or send letters to 7739 E. Broadway Blvd, #101, Tucson, AZ 85710-3941.

The Cowboy Soldier
Roz Denny Fox

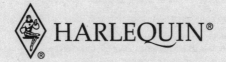

TORONTO • NEW YORK • LONDON
AMSTERDAM • PARIS • SYDNEY • HAMBURG
STOCKHOLM • ATHENS • TOKYO • MILAN • MADRID
PRAGUE • WARSAW • BUDAPEST • AUCKLAND

Recycling programs
for this product may
not exist in your area.

ISBN-13: 978-0-373-78393-9

THE COWBOY SOLDIER

www.eHarlequin.com

Printed in U.S.A.

ABOUT THE AUTHOR

Roz Denny Fox has been a RITA® Award finalist and has placed in a number of other contests; her books have also appeared on the Waldenbooks bestseller list. She's happy to have received her twenty-five-book pin with Harlequin Books and is steadily working toward one for fifty books. Roz worked for a number of years as medical record technician, and then for three pediatricians. She met her husband, Denny, when he was a marine, and they currently reside in Tucson, Arizona, a military town. They have two grown daughters.

Books by Roz Denny Fox

To my husband, Denny, who has been my biggest advocate and most loyal supporter from day one.

CHAPTER ONE

ALEXA ROBINSON SPOKE SOFTLY to the frisky black three-year-old gelding she worked on a lead rope. She'd bought this horse and a mare at a recent breeder's auction. Usually she gentled the horses she bought into smooth-gaited saddle mounts but she wouldn't have as much time to work with these. A former customer had said he'd buy the mare for his daughter, provided Alexa could train the horse for barrel racing by the girl's birthday in mid-December. It was now mid-October, which gave her just two months.

Autumn in the Chihuahuan Desert was dry. Her dog pounced on cottonwood fluff blowing inside the corral. Little puffs of dust flew up from the gelding's hooves as he danced at the end of the rope. Alexa took her eye off the border collie who stopped and perked his ears toward an aging green van that drove down her dirt road, creating larger dust plumes.

She had few visitors, and didn't recognize this vehicle. Her ranch was fairly remote, bordered as it was by the Chisos Mountains and the Big Bend National Park. Perhaps a previous customer had recommended her. That would be nice. If she could sell both new horses, the profit should get her through the winter.

The gelding snorted and pulled back as the van came to a dusty stop beside the corral. A dark-haired woman emerged, directing the four children inside to get out their crayons and coloring books. Retrieving a thick manila folder, the woman shut the driver's door and headed toward the corral.

Assuming she was lost and needed directions, Alexa unsnapped the rope from the gelding's halter. "May I help you?" she called, slipping out through the gate, making sure it latched securely behind her and the dog.

"I'm Sierra Martinez," the woman said, holding out a hand. "You're Dr. Robinson? I've come to discuss my brother, Rafe Eagle-feather. He was recently medically discharged from the army," she said, as if that clarified everything.

Alexa's smile vanished the instant the word

doctor passed the woman's lips. Withdrawing her gloved hand, she said, "I'm not a practicing doctor, Ms. Martinez."

"It's Mrs., but please call me Sierra. Aren't you an osteopath and an herbalist? I heard that at the feed store. And park rangers told my husband you've healed injured animals they've found in the park."

"Animals. Not people." Alexa hooked her coiled rope over a fence post before she said anything more. Almost angrily she stripped off one leather glove. The wind had dislodged strands of blond hair from her ponytail and she pushed them back behind her ear.

Creases formed between her visitor's solemn dark eyes. "My husband, Doug, is a border patrol agent. He told me you treated a pregnant woman—an illegal who was badly dehydrated. You kept her here and cared for her until you found her husband. Doug's partner also told me you set the broken arm of a little boy who fell during a border crossing."

"Those were emergencies. I had to act quickly. The nearest clinic is miles away." Alexa bent to pat Compadre who also eyed the stranger with misgiving. "The woman had been abandoned by the scoundrel she paid to bring her to Texas. She was malnourished and frightened. The boy…he cried without making a sound. It would have been cruel to make him travel to the clinic in such pain."

"My brother's a war hero," Sierra said with passionate emphasis. "Army doctors quit on Rafe and discharged him to family. To me. Doug and I have two sets of twins under age six. We all live in a two-bedroom house. Doug's building an addition, but it takes time. Meanwhile, Rafe's stuck sleeping in our living room. And I'm convinced he's being overmedicated. As for follow-up care, he's supposed to check in at a VA center in Houston or San Antonio once a week. The one time I drove him, we sat in the waiting room for hours, and they only added Valium to his other prescriptions. I can't make that trip weekly without putting a strain on my family. I'd hoped maybe he could stay here while you evaluate him. Maybe some natural methods can help him. Maybe they'll make him *want* to get better. Please. We can pay you."

Taken aback by the strange request and concerned that so many people knew about her, Alexa nevertheless felt sympathy for the distraught woman. "Money isn't the issue," she said. Although she'd been determined not to ask, she did. "Out of curiosity, what's wrong with your brother?"

"This is his medical record. All the information you need is here," Sierra Martinez thrust the fat manila folder she clutched into Alexa's hands.

A quick glimpse into the official chart of Rafe Eaglefeather showed Alexa that he'd been blinded after suffering a head injury when his patrol was hit by mortar fire. He'd also been shot in the leg during the same attack. The reference to the violent injury made Alexa think about Bobby Duval, her lifelong friend. One New Year's Eve he wrapped his Jeep around a tree after skidding on ice. E.R. doctors stopped his internal bleeding and removed his spleen. Even after he was released from the hospital, his treatments dragged on. Bobby had grown so weary of being poked and prodded. Alexa was willing to bet that Major Eaglefeather felt the same way.

"What do you think?" Sierra asked as Alexa leafed through the chart. "I've also included reports by some of Rafe's men. They said he fought hard trying to save his whole patrol. Not only was he shot and left blind, he lost his two best friends in the attack. The army gave him ribbons, medals and commendations, and the doctors gave him pills that are supposed to get him through the rest of his life. All they're doing is making him a zombie."

Though moved by accounts of the major's heroism, his apparent lack of will to be healed made Alexa pass the folder back to Sierra. "I'm sorry. I'm no miracle worker." Alexa tried to keep her voice steady, but her hands shook.

"Please. Do you have any idea how many veterans like Rafe fall through the cracks in our system? When my brother was discharged, the military doctor pulled me aside and mentioned how many commit suicide after they go home. It's shocking. I don't want my brother to be one of them." Her eyes filled.

Alexa spread her hands helplessly. "His case is tragic, I agree. But he needs MDs who are trained to treat the casualties of war."

"It's not Rafe's first tragedy," Sierra said, blotting her eyes on a sleeve. "When I was sixteen and Rafe fourteen, our parents died in a highway accident. I dropped out of school, got my GED and worked two jobs so we could eat and keep Rafe in school. Our folks wanted more for him than to farm and rodeo like our dad.

"Rafe graduated," she continued proudly. "He went to college and got a job caring for rodeo stock. Summers he rode in the circuit. He also crusaded to stiffen the rules governing the health of rodeo animals. Rafe loved horses more than winning buckles." Her eyes cut to the horse in Alexa's pen. "Rafe's dream was to own a ranch like yours when he retired from the army," she said softly.

Alexa knew Sierra was trying to play on her sympathies, but she was determined to stay strong. "How did he get from rodeos to the military, if you don't mind my asking?"

"Nine-eleven happened. Rafe and his two best friends from the rodeo joined the army. My brother was a good soldier. He pulled two tours in Iraq after basic training and was promoted several times before ending up in Afghanistan. It was the first time he and his friends landed in the same unit. Now Mike and Joey are dead, and I'm afraid Rafe wishes it'd been him instead."

Alexa knew all about guilt. It was the

reason she lived here at the ranch her grandfather had left her instead of running her practice in Houston. She'd needed solitude. And now that solitude was being threatened by the gut-wrenching pain in Sierra Martinez's eyes.

"What do you really know about holistic medicine?" Alexa asked abruptly.

"Our maternal grandmother was a *curandera*."

"Ah, a Hispanic healer. I trained with a Chinese herbalist, but I also work with native desert plants. They have many of the same properties as those used by the Chinese."

"My brother was a vital man once, but his spirit is dead. I believe there is a natural solution that won't kill his self-esteem—that won't mask who he is," Sierra declared, biting her trembling lower lip. "I'm confident you'll be able to help him."

"Do you have any family or friends living near a VA facility your brother could stay with while he gets treated?" Alexa felt herself weakening and tried to guard against it.

"No." Sierra hugged the dog-eared chart to her chest. "Since we lost our parents, it's been Rafe and me against the world. I know it's presumptuous to drop in on you. But he's my brother and I can't bear to see him like this."

Alexa's stomach tightened. As the only child of a busy oil tycoon, she used to long for a sibling. Her dad had had little time for her. Her mom had never understood her, and still didn't, even though she meant well. Alexa's compassion for people and animals came from tagging along after the veterinarian who looked after her father's extensive stable of race horses. And from a true, unconditional friendship with tough-talking, fun-loving Bobby Duval. He'd been like a brother.

Rubbing the V between her brows, she sighed. "I'll tell you what…if your brother agrees, and if he signs a release allowing alternative care, I'll consent to treat him on a thirty-day trial. He can help out on my ranch in trade. If he shows no improvement after a month, or if I think he's losing ground, I want a promise you'll help him move somewhere closer to a VA outpatient facility."

Sierra's face flooded with relief, and she nodded. She gave Alexa back the thick medical file. "Thank you, thank you, thank you. I know Rafe will agree. I'll bring him tomorrow after I drop my older twins at school. I'll pack the basics for him, but if you think of anything else he might need, you can always call me." Without waiting for Alexa's response, Sierra hurried to her van. Leaping in, she revved the engine and drove off amid plumes of dust so like the ones that had first caught Alexa's eye. Alexa choked on the billowing particles and wondered what in heaven's name she'd done.

RAFE EAGLEFEATHER STILL SAT in the same porch rocker he'd been sitting in when his sister left to run errands. He couldn't say how long she'd been away, except that a small pile of shavings had accumulated at his feet from the piece of wood he was whittling into a pony.

He felt the breeze and heard the footsteps of his sister's four kids as they scuttled silently past him to get into the house. That meant Sierra had stopped to collect Curt and Chloe from school. He let them go by without speaking to him. Both sets of twins had been born while he was out of the country, so they didn't really know him. Sierra had told them their uncle Rafe was blind and couldn't see to play games with them. Besides, that was the last thing he felt like doing.

"Hi, Rafe." Sierra sank into the chair beside him. "I'm sorry I was gone so long. I wish you wouldn't whittle when I'm not here."

"Doug gave me the wood," Rafe said, folding up his pocketknife.

"I know, but I worry you'll cut yourself. It looks like you've been at this project awhile. I'll get a broom and sweep up after I start supper."

He bent and tried to pick up the wood curls. "I know you asked me to use a waste basket in the house, but I figured the shavings would blow away out here."

"It's okay. Come inside. I need to make a meat loaf."

"You go ahead. I like being out in the fresh air." It was the truth, Rafe thought. "If I bought a cot, I could sleep out here on the porch."

He heard Sierra sigh.

"Oh, Rafe. I'm sorry you're stuck on the couch. Doug's been so busy he hasn't had much time to work on the addition."

"No problem, Sierra. I don't care where I sleep."

Rafe could sense his sister's hesitation in the short pause that followed.

"Uh, Rafe, I need to talk to you about something," she said at last.

Whatever it was, Rafe realized, his sister was worried that he wouldn't like it.

"There's a healer who lives a couple of hours away," she continued. "A woman. She uses herbs in place of pharmaceuticals. I went to meet her and had her look at your medical report to get her opinion. She's nice, Rafe, and lives on a ranch with horses."

Sierra was speaking to him the way she would to her children, Rafe thought. He felt a gentle hand rest on his knee.

"Her name is Dr. Robinson. She's willing to work with you for a month—see if she can help you get off those antidepressants. What do you think?"

He thought that Sierra just couldn't seem to accept that he'd be like this for the rest of his life.

"Say something, dammit!" Sierra pulled back and withdrew her hand from him.

"Say what?" Rafe asked.

"The old Rafe would tell me to stop meddling in his life. Where's your spunk? It's your life, your future I'm trying to save, Rafe."

He knew his lack of response frustrated his kind-hearted sister, but there was nothing he could do to change that.

"I'll go if you want me to," he said. "But the truth is…I couldn't see in Houston. I can't see here. That's my future, Sierra."

"No it isn't. You're only thirty-five. That's why I want you to see this doctor. You have a lot of years ahead of you and I'm going to do everything I can to make them good ones."

Rafe made no comment to that.

Sierra touched the collar of his shirt, then she kissed his cheek. "I'm going inside. Doug should be home soon. I know he'll want to eat and try to do some framing on the addition while there's still daylight. We'll go to Dr. Robinson's tomorrow after I drop Curt and Chloe off at kindergarten. I'll see if Doug's sister is available to watch Maris and Melina for a few hours. They'd go crazy cooped up in car seats for such a long drive."

"They're good kids, Sierra. I hear you tell them not to bother me but I wish you wouldn't. This is their home. I'm the intruder."

"Never. You're family. And if you think

I'm shuffling you off to Alexa Robinson's to get rid of you, that's simply not true. I'm praying you'll come back the old Rafe."

"That'll take a miracle."

"Then I'll say novenas."

"A novena only runs nine days. The military docs worked on me six months."

"Dr. Robinson is giving you one month. So I'll do three novenas."

Rafe heard the screen door slam, so obviously she'd missed his shrug. Bless her heart. Sierra refused to believe he really didn't give a damn.

BY LATE AFTERNOON the next day, Alexa was prepared to take Sierra Martinez aside and tell her she'd made a mistake. How would it look to customers coming to see about horses or the park rangers who occasionally brought her sick animals if they found her living alone with a patient. Or even if word got around that she was treating human patients. She'd been hurt by lies and rumors once and didn't want to go through that again.

Alexa had her speech ready but didn't have a chance to get a word out. Sierra hit the ground talking.

"You told me Rafe had to agree to come," she said, shoving a worn khaki duffel bag at Alexa. "He did. And here's his stuff. This should do him for a couple of weeks. I'll come by then and pick up his laundry and bring him fresh clothes to make it easier on you. Oh, my number's programmed in his cell phone speed dial if you need me. I don't think I've left out anything, but you never know." She hugged the man standing next to her, then vaulted back into the van as if she couldn't get away fast enough.

"Wait!" Alexa frowned down at the duffel in her hands.

"By the way," Sierra called out, "I put his electric razor in the bottom of the bag. Oh, and his pills. Too many of those. Anti-anxiety, sedatives and something else. I hope you'll wean him off them before long." With a bright smile and a wave, she shut the car door and motored off.

"Well," Alexa drawled. "Here we are, two strangers—plus a dog." Compadre trotted up and sniffed Rafe's boots then snuffled his hand. "Compadre is a border collie, a stray who adopted me. Or we adopted each other. I hope you like animals. I have quite a few on this ranch." Alexa realized she was babbling and bit down hard on her lower lip. Truthfully, she was bowled over by Rafe Eaglefeather's good looks. She'd read his medical history last night and knew he was thirty-five to her thirty, and she'd probably read his height and weight. But statistics were nothing compared to the real man. The major was tall, raven-haired and golden-eyed, and he put Alexa in mind of a proud, wounded bird—like his namesake the eagle.

And those eyes. She'd assumed they'd be unfocused, or even injured. Instead, he stared straight at her when she spoke, and it was downright unnerving. Could he be *faking?* Impossible. He'd been examined by countless doctors.

She gave herself a little shake. They couldn't just stand here all day.

"Uh, let's get you settled." Gripping the handles of his duffel, Alexa directed him up to the house and opened the screen door with her free hand. "Your bedroom is this way." She tugged on his arm.

Rafe stumbled over the dog.

"Ooh!"

Alexa dropped the bag and managed

to catch him, but he was heavier than she thought. They both almost went down.

But the near fall proved he wasn't faking. Nor had the man gone soft since he'd left the military. He was six feet of solid male. His deep, gravelly, "Sorry," as he attempted to untangle himself from Alexa's grasp sent a tingle up her arm.

She shrugged it off. What woman wouldn't react to such a terrific-looking guy? Sierra had made it plain she was his only family, but a man this good-looking probably had a string of girlfriends. Alexa sneaked another sidelong peek at him as she hesitantly took his elbow and guided him through the kitchen and down the hall to his room.

"Oh, I have a paper I need signed by you. A release for treatment. I intended to read it aloud while your sister was still here so she could vouch for what it says."

Alexa expected him to comment. He said nothing.

"The release sets out the terms of treatment. It's important we both agree to them." They'd reached his room. "This is where you'll stay," she said, directing him inside.

He gave a casual shrug as they entered his

room. "Give me a pen and set my hand down where I have to sign."

"Okay. But one thing I need to make clear is that you will relinquish all your prescription medications to me, and I'll decide how and when to dispense them."

"No problem. There should be four bottles of pills in my duffel."

She leaned down and dug them out, wincing at what she saw. "Okay, this is your bed." Alexa shoved the pills in her pockets before placing his palm on the quilt. "There's a three-drawer chest with a lamp next to the bed. It'll be on your right as you're lying down."

She saw the slight curl of his lip at the mention of a lamp. Too bad. She was responsible for his safety while he was here.

"I know you can't see, Major, but I'd prefer to leave a light on when you're in here except when you're sleeping," she said. "It'll help me. Now come this way. I'll let you count the steps to the attached bath. It has a walk-in shower, a sink and commode." When he said nothing, she counted the steps for him as she led the way. "Four steps left of the bathroom door is a closet." The two of them made a full circuit of the room, arriving at a wicker chair that she made Rafe touch. From there she counted the steps back to his bed. "This room's decor is red and white with some browns and golds. Nothing feminine. Western motif."

He simply stood with his arms dangling loosely at his sides.

So that's the way it was going to be. "I just thought you'd like to know. You don't seem like a man who'd want to be stuck in a room with frills."

"I told the army docs, and I told Sierra," Rafe said, not altering his stance. "Now I'm telling you. I don't give a rat's ass where I spend my time. You, Sierra, the VA—the whole lot of you can do whatever you want with me." His jaw tensed and he fisted his hands at his sides.

Compadre whined and pawed Rafe's knee a few times.

Alexa hadn't studied a lot of psychology, but she knew pent-up rage mixed with guilt when she saw it. Her inclination was to leave him alone to stew, but her compassion over-ruled the uncharitable thought.

"I'll help you put away your clothes, then I'll leave you alone awhile to get comfort-able with your new digs." As she spoke she pulled stuff out of the duffel and saw that he'd come with precious little. Several pair of worn fatigues, underwear and an assortment of colored T-shirts. "Where shall I put your boots?"

"What boots?" he asked.

"There's a second set of…combat boots, I guess you call them. Like the ones you have on." Alexa held them out so he could trace a finger over the leather.

"I have no idea what Sierra sent." He picked up the bag and dumped the remaining contents on the bed. "What the…?" He shook a plastic bag filled with military medals, and a second one with rodeo buckles. "Useless," he said, his voice strained.

"Why don't I just put them in a dresser drawer. Your sister is extremely proud of you, you know. She loves you." Alexa smiled even though Rafe couldn't see.

"Hell! I know that."

A reaction at last!

Just as quickly, his face became impassive again. "Do what you want with that stuff. Toss it in the trash for all I care. Where's that damned paper you want me to sign? Let's get it done, so I don't take up any more of your valuable time, Doctor."

"All right. I'll go get the form from my office, Major. Be right back."

"I'm no longer a major. That's over and done with. Call me Rafe."

Two could play this game. "If you call me Alexa. Lately my practice has consisted of a pair of young mountain lions, a great-horned owl, a family of squirrels and other assorted forest animals. I'm not used to being called by my title."

"Sierra said you're a healer. I thought you were a *curandera* like our grandmother Velasquez, but it sounds like you're a vet."

"No, I'm not a vet or a *curandera*. I'm an osteopath, and I hold certificates in Chinese herbs and acupuncture."

He twisted his mouth to one side. "So you stick needles in people. Guess it can't be any worse than what they put me through in the field hospital."

Alexa wasn't sure if Rafe was trying to be funny or sarcastic. Whatever. He definitely presented a challenge—one that intrigued her.

She headed down the hall to her office,

which was located off her bedroom at the opposite end of the house. She had always liked this split floor plan. The few summers her parents had brought her here to visit her grandparents, she'd had the room Rafe now occupied. As a teen she'd pretended this whole end of the house was all her domain. Mostly, she holed up there reading biographies of female scientists who'd changed the world. At the time she wore chunky braces and round black-rimmed glasses, which explained why she didn't read romances and dream about boys like her mother wanted her to do. Bobby was the only boy who ever really saw through her serious facade. And even he liked her best for her brain.

Grabbing the release form she'd printed out the night before, she went back to Rafe's room. He had drawn the blinds, making the room dark, and sat in the chair, petting Compadre. If dogs could smile, the collie gave a great imitation.

"Here's the release," she said. "It's attached to a clipboard." She started to read the outline of treatment but Rafe raised his hand.

"Just the part about the pills," he said.

Alexa did as he asked and read the short

statement giving her the right to wean him off his pills and instead use herbs, teas and Eastern techniques such as acupuncture with Rafe's verbal agreement.

He took the pen and scribbled his name.

"Dinner's at six," she told him. "I'll give you plenty of time to wash up. I thought I'd put a couple of steaks on the grill and make a salad with vegetables from my garden. Lettuce, if the rabbits and deer left me any, tomatoes and cucumbers." She let the words hang, expecting his agreement and maybe a little enthusiasm or interest.

"I don't want anything to eat."

"Well, at least come out and learn how to navigate the rest of the house."

"No, I prefer to stay here."

Alexa struggled to remain patient. "Okay, suit yourself tonight. But even if you're not hungry, there's a hot mineral springs on the property. It's therapeutic and you'd be amazed at how relaxed you'll feel if you take a dip right before bedtime. I'd go with you, of course."

He shook his head. "Not interested. I plan to turn in early."

Alexa began to simmer. But he was the

patient and she was the doctor, she reminded herself. "Tomorrow, then. We'll get a fresh start. If Compadre makes a nuisance of himself, boot him out and shut your door."

Hearing his name, the dog sat up, whined a few times, then laid his furry chin on Rafe's knee. Alexa watched the man stroke the animal's silky ears. "He's fine," Rafe said in a quiet voice. "I had a dog as a boy. A mongrel. We had to give him away when my parents died. Couldn't afford to feed him. Chip. That was his name. I haven't thought about him in years."

He looked so vulnerable sitting there, steeped in memories of the pet he'd lost, and Alexa found her throat tightening in sympathy. Her reaction was totally at odds with the irritation she'd felt barely a minute ago. "I'll, uh, go now, and check back later to see if you need anything. Oh, I forgot. There's a small fridge in the closet. I wasn't sure what drinks you liked, but I left a couple of bottles of water, a fruit juice and non-caffeinated soft drinks."

"Beer?" He turned toward her.

"Sorry, alcohol doesn't mix with all those high-velocity meds you already took today.

But that's something we can shoot for. Call it a carrot to wean you off those psychotropic drugs."

"Psycho-what?"

"Sorry, doctor speak for antidepressants and the like."

"Oh." He sank back in the chair and closed his eyes. A sign their conversation, such as it was, had come to an end.

Alexa hurried down the hall, her mind already cataloging the herbs that might work as substitutes to help him start withdrawing from the most potent of his drugs.

After eating a salad by herself, she went into her office and pulled out the notes she'd made on Rafe's current course of treatment. She skimmed them then sat down at the computer and searched the Internet for information on returning soldiers. A number of them came home suffering intermittent bouts of deafness from unspecified causes. But almost all cases of blindness could be traced to IED explosions that left shrapnel buried in the head. Rafe's physical exams, including extensive X-rays and MRIs, revealed no foreign objects other than bullets in his left shoulder and thigh, both of which had been removed.

Alexa tapped a pencil to her lips. She wondered if anyone was studying the residual effects of severe concussion around the brain.

She flipped back to the detailed account of the firefight given by a young private— one of six men Rafe pulled to safety while he took and returned fire. Apparently saving half his patrol wasn't good enough for Rafe Eaglefeather. He was the type of guy who'd feel guilty for not saving them all.

Alexa could relate to that.

Feeling weepy for no good reason, she shut down her computer and got ready for bed. She crawled under the covers, and it struck her that for the first time since she'd nursed Compadre back to health, he'd abandoned her for Rafe. Really, she didn't mind. Dogs intuitively sensed which human needed the most attention.

In the middle of the night, Alexa heard loud shouting.

Rafe.

Bolting out of bed, she wrapped herself in her silk bathrobe and stumbled down the hall. Had he fallen on his way to the bathroom?

Halfway to his room she heard Compadre whining.

The bedroom door stood ajar and she could hear Rafe thrashing about, shouting men's names, urging them to find cover and protect their heads. His medical file had noted episodes of post-traumatic stress flashback. Aware how violent some PTSD patients got, Alexa debated whether or not to enter his room. She had withheld his sedatives that night. Had it been a mistake?

Still, he was under her care. She cracked the door wider. Thanks to a huge harvest moon filtering through the upper portion of one tall window, she saw Rafe sit up, shudder, and rub his forehead with the heels of his palms. Then he spoke softly to the anxious collie, who had both front paws on the bed.

Relieved to feel her own pounding heart settle, Alexa continued to hover, unsure if she should announce her presence. The doctor in her argued yes. But she went with her feminine instincts. A macho, tough-guy like Rafe would be embarrassed to have anyone, especially a woman, witness what he would perceive as a weakness.

As the dog quieted and settled back down

on the floor beside Rafe, she withdrew and stealthily pulled the door closed behind her.

Unfortunately, she was too keyed up to sleep. After witnessing Rafe's flashback, she realized she needed to focus more on alleviating his stress and tension than researching old Chinese remedies for blindness, so she went to her office and started making a list of restorative therapies. Lists made order of chaotic feelings.

But what if she got it wrong? What if her treatments made no difference, or God forbid, made Rafe worse?

After long hours of research, Alexa felt certain that the approach she'd come up with would do him no harm.

Around 4:00 a.m. she crawled back into bed, but her mind was filled with a new worry. Healing could happen only if the patient had the will to make it happen. And the million-dollar question was, did Rafe Eaglefeather really want to get well?

CHAPTER TWO

AT APPROXIMATELY SIX, after only a couple of hours of sleep, Alexa bustled about her kitchen fixing breakfast. Her mind mulled over possible chores Rafe might do. From his file she knew that he'd been sedentary in the months before his discharge, and she had a feeling that Sierra wouldn't have pushed him to exert himself. But Alexa had no intention of letting him waste his mind or that finely honed body.

Compadre padded into the kitchen and went straight to his kibble bowl.

"Hey, boy. Is your new friend up and around?" Alexa moved a pot of oatmeal to a back burner and glanced expectantly down the hall. Rafe wasn't in sight, and she couldn't hear the shower or other sounds of him moving about.

Deciding she'd better check on him, she cracked open his door and saw he was still lying in bed. "Rise and shine," she hollered. "Breakfast is ready and we have chores waiting."

A muffled "Go away" came from under his pillow.

"What is the army term for get your butt out of bed, soldier? Sorry I don't have a bugle. If you didn't bring an alarm, I'll give you one for tomorrow."

"You're pushing your luck, Doc." Rafe's voice sounded raspy. "I didn't sleep well last night."

"Neither did I. The animals out in the barns don't care. They need to be fed and watered." Alexa pushed the door wider, strode across the room and yanked off Rafe's covers. She immediately wished she hadn't. Rafe Eagle-feather slept in the raw.

"What in hell do you think you're doing?" Rafe's head popped out from under the pillow, which he hastily jerked down to cover his privates.

Alexa's heart wrenched at the sight of the red scars marring the bronze flesh of Rafe's hip. A second scar ran from his rib cage to what looked like a bullet exit wound near his collarbone, just below his right shoulder.

She steeled herself against uttering the sympathetic retort that came automatically. She didn't think Rafe would appreciate it.

"The oatmeal is getting cold," she said. "I'll be back in fifteen minutes to show you the way to the kitchen. Call me if you need me." Before she left she headed over to the window and threw open the curtains with unsteady hands.

Rafe winced, so she knew his eyes were sensitive to light.

He scowled. "I'm a civilian now, and I don't have to take orders from you or anybody."

"Oh yes, you do. For the next thirty days, unless you call your sister to come get you, you're my patient. Put simply, that means I outrank you, Major." Alexa walked out, Rafe's succinct expletive echoing behind her.

THE DOOR SLAMMED SO HARD Rafe heard it click and bounce back open again. He sat for a minute contemplating if he would continue to resist or just give in. His roar had sent seasoned military nurses skittering from his room, but it didn't seem to faze Dr. Robinson.

He swung his legs off the bed and counted the steps to the chair where he'd left his clothes. He couldn't help but be intrigued by her. She was a woman who spoke with a velvet voice but acted with hardfisted resolve.

Pulling on the clothes he'd worn yesterday, Rafe wondered if Alexa had flinched at the sight of his scars. Even though he'd never seen them himself, he knew they weren't pretty. He had that on good authority from several battle-hardened nurses who had changed his bandages after each series of surgeries. And within his hearing, doctors had discussed his wounds in gory detail.

But why in hell did it matter to him if Alexa Robinson had recoiled or not? No woman was going to look at him now with anything but pity.

This was not the first time since he'd woken up in a field hospital alive but blind that Rafe regretted he wasn't one of the lucky soldiers who had a wife waiting at home. A loyal, loving wife. Several guys in his shot-up unit had wives who were just glad to see them come home. Rafe didn't want to, but at a gut level, he envied those men.

If he wasn't careful, he mused, making sure he had gotten his shirt on with the tag at the back, he might start imagining Dr. Robinson as a possible candidate. God, but she smelled good enough to eat. Or did he think that because he'd had his fill of medicinal smells and the acrid odor of war? When a man lived too long in rough surroundings, he lost touch with the gentler things in life. But the few times Alexa had come and gone from his room, he hadn't missed the clean, summery scent she left in her wake.

He gave himself a hard mental shake. As far as he was concerned, the doctor was being a hard/ass, and he'd better keep it at that.

ALEXA WAITED THE FULL fifteen minutes. She started down the hall, but stopped when she saw Rafe emerge from his bedroom. He walked slowly and with an odd gait because he kept one hand resting atop Compadre's furry head.

"There you are," she called over her shoulder as she beat a hasty retreat and waited for them in the kitchen.

"Yeah, Dog is as persistent as you are," Rafe muttered.

"I named him Compadre. He's more like a friend than the other animals I doctor back to health. He's been with me almost a year. I pulled him half drowned from the Rio Grande when it flooded. I asked the park rangers to put out the word to try to find his owner, but no one came forward. He seems to like living here."

Rafe merely grunted.

She pulled out a chair. "Here, have a seat at the kitchen table."

Rafe grasped the chair back and awkwardly felt his way around the cushioned seat until he seemed sure enough of his bearings to sit.

Alexa picked up a teapot. "I'm pouring you some tea."

"I prefer coffee."

"Tea has greater healing properties. If you think of your plate as a clock, I set your mug at two o'clock. It's quite hot, so be careful."

Alexa anxiously watched Rafe pick up the sturdy mug and take a sip.

He promptly gagged. "What the hell? Are you trying to poison me?" Rafe set the mug down with a thump that sloshed tea over his hand. "Ow, dammit." With a mutinous look, he raised his burned fingers to his lips.

Grabbing an ice cube out of the freezer, Alexa made him hold it on the rapidly reddening web between his thumb and forefinger. "I probably should have warned you I'd brewed tea from wood betony and basil today. It's very therapeutic." She purposely didn't tell him she'd chosen those herbs to help him cope with stress. She knew from former male patients, that men shied from any suggestion they might have mental or emotional problems.

"Therapeutic or not, it tastes like shit. If I can't have coffee, I'll drink water."

"But the herbs in the tea will help you... regain strength," she finally said.

"Strength isn't what I'm lacking. I've lost my sight. No damn tea is gonna help me see again. Where's the oatmeal you said was ready? At least that should taste normal."

At the stove, Alexa paused. She'd already stirred in a small amount of lemon balm and vervain tincture into the hot cereal, although oats alone were thought to act as a minor antidepressant. She tasted the mixture, made a face and quickly sprinkled brown sugar over the portion she'd spooned into Rafe's bowl.

"I'll take mine with milk—good old cow's milk. We had goat's milk in Afghanistan— talk about rank."

"Uh, milk. Just a minute." Alexa quickly

removed the small pitcher of warm goat's milk from the table and rummaged in the refrigerator for the carton of regular milk she'd bought on her last trip into town. She sniffed it to make sure it hadn't spoiled.

"Here's some nonfat. Sierra didn't mention you were such a picky eater."

"Nonfat?" he parroted. "So, I guess you're on a diet."

"No way." Alexa unconsciously ran a hand down her slender hips. "Why on earth would you think that?" she asked rather huffily as she dumped milk on his oatmeal and stuck a spoon in his hand.

He hiked up one shoulder. "Sierra switched to one-percent milk after her pediatrician said too many American kids are overweight."

"True. But in my case, nonfat has a longer shelf life. I don't go to town often."

Rafe ate a few bites of the cereal, then lifted his head. Alexa held her breath, waiting for him to complain about the taste of the oatmeal. Instead, he said, "It took Sierra a long time to get here once we left the highway, so your place must be really off the beaten track. What's the story behind that?"

"The story?" Alexa scrambled for something to say. She wasn't about to bring up Bobby, so instead, she settled on part of the truth. "My grandparents owned this ranch, so it was only logical for me to take it over. My primary occupation is gentling horses to sell to families who want a well-trained saddle horse. I think I mentioned the hot springs my grandparents discovered here. That's another plus. My grandfather had degenerative arthritis and the springs were therapeutic for him. The area's perfect for me because it's so sparsely settled and the herbs that grow around here are uncontaminated. I gather native plants in my spare time."

Rafe scarfed down the rest of his oatmeal, and swallowed the pill she handed him before he stood. "It's really none of my business. Your life, I mean. I shouldn't have been so nosy." Dropping his napkin on the table, he waved a hand in the air around him and seemed noticeably relieved when Compadre trotted up to head-butt his fingers.

"Where are you going?" Alexa asked, quickly finishing her own oatmeal. "Give me a minute to rinse our dishes and stick them in the dishwasher, then we'll go feed my menagerie."

"I'm going back to my room."

She pursed her lips. "There's a three-quarter bath off the kitchen if you need to use the facilities before we go out to the barns."

"I don't need the bathroom."

"Then wait here a minute. It's closer to the barns if we go out the back door."

"What do you expect me to do there?" Rafe asked churlishly. "You know darned well I can't see spit. I'll be in my room until you call me for lunch." He started off, Compadre at his side.

Feeling a prick of sorrow, Alexa was inclined to let him go. But to do what? There was nothing worse for him than to sit around all day with nothing to occupy his mind but the loss of his eyesight. So she forced herself to toughen her heart. "Hold it right there, Major. Horses pay the bills and put food on the table at this ranch. If you plan to eat three squares a day for the next month, you'll pull your weight around here."

"Did Sierra ask what your services cost? I'll pay for my keep."

"I don't want your money. I want you to stop acting like an invalid."

ANGER BOILED IN THE PIT of Rafe's stomach at Alexa's high-handedness. He could follow her out to the barns and fail miserably, proving his point. Or he could call Sierra to come get him and end this stupid charade. Then he thought about Sierra. How she'd placed so much faith in his coming here. He'd worried her enough already and wouldn't add to the burden. "Okay, Doc. You win another round. We'll try it your way today." He swung back toward the table, but knocked over the chair where he'd been sitting, and instantly froze.

Compadre started to bark and dance around his legs, and Rafe didn't know which way to turn. He was furious at being so clumsy, and the anger he'd already directed toward Alexa Robinson for putting him in such an untenable position doubled.

He realized she was speaking to him, calmly telling him where the fallen chair was in relation to his left foot. "If you bend your knees and put out your left hand, you'll feel the chair back, and you can set it upright."

Rafe followed Alexa's instructions, shocked that she didn't rush right over and pick up the chair for him, which was what would've happened with the hospital nurses or Sierra and Doug. Once he had the chair on solid footing, he felt a rare sense of accomplishment, the first he'd experienced since his injury. "Thanks," he said gruffly, begrudgingly giving Alexa a sliver of respect. "I hate the way everyone treats me like a cripple. It's almost worse than being sent home with a medal while buddies I should've saved came home in caskets."

"The term used now is *disabled,* not crippled. And I have high expectations for you." Alexa placed a couple of items in his hands. "Slip on these sunglasses and we'll be on our way. You'll need the gloves in the barn. Count how many steps it takes you to get to the barn from the back door. Counting steps and remembering the number puts you on the first rung of the ladder to independence, Major."

That put her up another notch on Rafe's judgment scale. "I recall asking you to call me Rafe. I was discharged from the army months ago."

"Okay, but then don't call me Doc. I've never been one of the seven dwarfs."

Rafe cracked a partial smile. "You got me there."

They exited the house with Dog, Alexa pro-

viding running commentary about the land-
scape.

Interest in what she was saying kept Rafe
placing one foot in front of the other until
she announced, "This is it. We're at the first
and smaller of my two barns. This is where
I house the wildlife that park rangers find
in their travels and bring to me. That started
after I pulled over on the road one day to help
a fawn someone had hit. The ranger dropped
by to see how the fawn made out and found
her well enough to return to the wild." He felt
her touch his arm. "On your left is the corral
I use to train three-year-old horses I buy from
an area breeder. The horse barn is eighty to
a hundred steps behind this one, and sits at
the edge of the woods, which is the end of
my property. Next to the horse barn, I have
a chicken coop and a pen for...uh, other do-
mestic animals."

Rafe wondered why she sounded hesitant,
but decided not to ask. He took a deep breath
and felt the tightness in his chest ease. "The
air smells of horses and a whiff of cedar. It
sorta reminds me of home. Sierra and I grew
up in Terlingua, west of here."

His words stoked memories of the carefree

days when Mike, Joey and he rode bucking broncs to the buzzer all summer long.
Afterward, the three of them enjoyed cold
brewskies at a local bar. Whichever man
walked out with the prettiest girl had to pay
the tab. But, his buddies were dead. His fault.
He'd been their leader, after all.

By this time, Alexa had led him into the
barn, and suddenly, Rafe found it impossible
to breathe.

Pungent air, thick with the aroma of earth
and animal dung, set his head spinning. The
clang of metal on metal as the door banged
closed behind them shot him straight back to
the last trek he'd made through the Afghan
mountains. That sound meant one thing—
bullets striking their equipment jeep. Familiar earthy smells of goats and the unwashed
bodies of the men who tended the flocks
threatened to choke him. Innocent looking
goat tenders often hid automatic weapons
under their worn robes. His body rigid, Rafe
was sure he could smell goat, and he started
to shake. His patrol should take cover. Where
were they?

Someone was touching his arm, and a quiet
voice said, "You're fine, Rafe. This is Texas.

As soon as we finish feeding all the stock, we'll go soak away your anxiety at the hot springs. If that's not enough, I'll throw in a peppermint-oil back massage afterward. I know yesterday you nixed the idea of a trip to the springs, but I guarantee, once you step into the water, you'll be hooked forever."

Her voice ricocheted like gunshots inside Rafe's head. Desperate to flee, to find his patrol, he wheeled and tripped over an empty feed bucket and went sprawling. The clatter of his boot on the tin bucket sent the animals around him into a frenzy. He could hear a mountain lion hiss and snarl, and a great owl hooted and flapped its wings. Squirrels chattered nonstop and he heard the shriek of a hawk.

The animals must be warning him of an impending attack. Rafe grabbed Alexa's legs and threw her down on the ground. He flung an arm over her torso and barked a series of staccato orders. "Don't move a muscle. Let the heavy artillery rout out the enemy."

"Easy," a soothing voice whispered. "You're okay. Breathe deeply."

Gradually his pounding heart slowed to a normal rate, and he heard the gentle patter of an animal's paws approaching just seconds before a wet tongue lapped his face.

Rafe was aware that he was emerging from a flashback. Part of him understood that the threat hadn't been real. But a major portion of his brain was still befuddled. It made no sense that his face was buried in long strands of sweet-smelling hair. Again, a bird squawked in the background, and it rattled Rafe all the more when a woman shifted out from under him, sat up and forced him to do the same. What were they doing on the ground? *Dr. Robinson. God, had he attacked her?*

"Are you okay?" she murmured. "You had a small flashback, Rafe."

The question had him sweating profusely. Was he getting worse? He hadn't had a single flashback at Sierra's. This was his second since coming here.

"You fell over a feed bucket," Alexa said, scrambling to her knees as she began calmly checking his face and arms for cuts or bruises. "It was my fault. I saw the bucket, but didn't move it out of the aisle. Feed buckets belong on wall pegs, not on the barn floor where they can trip people. I swear I'll be more careful in the future."

Her cool, seductive touch telegraphed a signal to Rafe's body. Even though he couldn't see the woman who hovered so close to him, he was still a man. All man.

His fingers flexed around Alexa's upper arms and he pulled her forward until he could feel the outline of her soft breasts against his chest. It frustrated him to not be able to see her face—her lips. He knew they parted invitingly, because he felt her gasp, and tiny puffs of her sweet breath tickled his mouth. His grip tightened as he savored the thought of how those soft lips would taste.

"Rafe?" She wedged her hands between them, pushing his chest gently, but firmly. "You're still hallucinating. I'm your doctor. You're my patient. Snap out of it, Major."

The embarrassment of the situation slammed hard into Rafe. *What was he doing?* Disgusted with himself, he dropped Alexa's arms like they were torches of fire.

"This whole idea of me helping you feed your animals is stupid," he shouted. "It's obvious I'm totally useless." He struggled to get to his feet, and when he was upright, he ordered, "Take me back to my room. Right now."

He heard Alexa lift something down from the barn wall.

"I'll clip a leash to Compadre's collar," she said in a neutral voice. "If you want to go to the house, let him lead you. I happen to have chores to finish."

Rafe wound the loop of leather around his wrist, and although he'd been stung by Alexa's taunt, he followed the dog out into the fresh air.

Only after he was inside his bedroom did he allow himself to acknowledge his shame. Not so much for the flashback. He had no control over those. But he had turned tail and bailed on Alexa. One thing Rafe had never been was a quitter.

For an hour he paced the room, trying to think of a way to redeem himself with Alexa. He had hated lying around, useless in the hospital. And he'd been in the way at Sierra's. Alexa was the first person who seemed to believe he could be independent. If he stopped being pigheaded and listened to her, maybe he could learn to live on his own. That appealed to Rafe. Prior to the debacle in the barn, he'd felt invigorated. Sierra believed his loss of sight was caused by a block to his brain. He wasn't so sure about that himself, but maybe if he started depending more on himself than on others, he could eventually function on his own, as Alexa believed.

Rafe wondered if she was the kind of woman who needed to make a man grovel for forgiveness. He didn't grovel well. On the other hand, he wasn't above turning on a little charm to see if that would get him a second chance.

ALEXA FELT A LITTLE GUILTY at dredging up busy work in order not to go back to the house until suppertime. Professionally, she knew patients sometimes hit on their doctors. And Rafe had been suffering some type of flashback. But the real problem lay with her. She found Rafe attractive. And she wasn't a desperate woman living in an isolated area. One park ranger in particular had hinted he was interested in her romantically, and she'd ignored him without a problem.

But she'd come within inches of kissing Rafe. There was no question about it, though— getting involved with Rafe would be ethically wrong and violate doctor-patient trust. In any case, Rafe had undoubtedly been thinking of some other woman today when he'd reached for her. Someone from his past. Or maybe he'd just been looking for comfort. Right now he was probably regretting coming here and packing his duffel to leave the ranch. But no matter what he decided, her professional code of conduct was intact. No romantic fraternizing with the former major, regardless of how compelling a man he was.

Shortly before dark, she entered her house through the back door and found Rafe and Compadre standing in front of the open fridge. Guilt rose up in her.

"I'm sorry, but I got tied up cleaning stalls. Time just got away from me," she fibbed.

"No problem," Rafe said lightly. "As you pointed out this morning, this is a working ranch. Care and feeding of stock comes first." He shut the fridge door. "I thought maybe I could fix us an easy meal. Maybe soup and cheese sandwiches." His shoulders drooped slightly. "But, I couldn't find bread *or* cheese. I feel bad for being here and causing you extra work."

So he wasn't going to mention the incident in the barn, Alexa thought. Well, neither would she. "I came in fully expecting you might have phoned Sierra to come pick you up."

Rafe crossed his arms and leaned on the counter. "The truth is, I like it here. I especially like the fact that you don't take any crap from me. I want to learn to do things for myself again. Can we start over tomorrow—on a better footing?"

He looked so boyishly contrite, an errant black curl or two falling down over his forehead, that Alexa couldn't have refused his request if she'd wanted to. "That sounds good to me." She figured she might have to rethink her approach. "Give me time to shower, then you can help me fix soup and grilled cheese sandwiches."

"Sure, but I figured you'd want to soak in that hot spring you keep talking about."

"Another day. We both skipped lunch. Compadre cleaned his dish, I see." Alexa picked up the empty bowl and took a bag of kibble from a cupboard. She thrust both into Rafe's hands. "There's a cup in this sack. Put two cups full of dry dog food in this dish and set it on the rubber mat on the floor across from the fridge. Compadre will thank you and so will I. Fifteen minutes. Twenty, max, and I'll be back." She hurried into the office that sat adjacent to the kitchen and led to her rooms, ignoring the anticipation surging through her.

The rest of the evening went off without incident. Neither she nor Rafe made any reference to what had happened earlier. Rafe was the first to head off to bed.

"I found you an alarm clock," Alexa told him. "It's set for seven." She passed the clock to Rafe. "I'll go out at six and feed the wild animals, then come back and make breakfast. I've been thinking that working with the horses will probably suit you best."

"I used to have a real rapport with horses," Rafe told her. "Of course, back then I could look one in the eye and show him who was boss."

Alexa refused to let herself respond to the regret in his voice. Hope and confidence were important tools in the medical arsenal, both for doctor and patient. "Rome wasn't built in a day," she said. "We'll go slow. Being active restores energy, so the work will be good for you. I've got some new herbal combinations I think you should try."

"Just so you know…I'm not drinking any

more of that crap tea. It tasted like dirty dishwater."

Alexa laughed. "I'm planning to brew up a little skullcap and passionflower tea tomorrow."

"I hope you're kidding." Rafe shuddered as he left the kitchen.

ALEXA HADN'T BEEN TEASING.

Rafe chugged down a full cup of tea the next morning but said nothing. And he seemed in better spirits when the two of them, with Compadre, started for the horse barn.

"Are you raising a particular breed of horse?" Rafe asked.

"Andalusian."

"I've never worked with any of those. But horses are horses, right?"

"I chose the Spanish breed for several reasons. They're tall, strong and intelligent, and have a good temperament. Most of my clients want gentle riding horses. I buy two or three at a time from a reputable breeder. Mares and geldings. I gentle them over time, and get them used to trail rides. But one of the mares I have now needs to be trained as a barrel racer."

"Really?" Rafe appeared interested. They entered the large barn, and this time there were no flashbacks. The mare she'd mentioned, named Esperanza, whinnied and nuzzled Rafe's neck the minute Alexa led her out of her stall.

"I think she likes you." Alexa clipped a rope to the mare's halter and handed the lead line to Rafe. "You want to take her into the corral? Put her through her paces?"

"You'd trust me to do that?"

"It's a big, bare dirt corral. I showed you where it is. Give it a whirl. I'll feed my saddle horses, then pop out to see how you're getting along before I take Tano, Esperanza's brother, into the smaller exercise pen." She handed him a pair of sunglasses and reminded him to cover his eyes before she opened the double doors that led into the corral. "You need to protect your eyes from sunburn since you can't tell how bright or intense the sun actually is."

The mare pranced out into the sunshine, forcing Rafe to jog out, too. Alexa kept Compadre from getting under his feet.

Standing just inside the barn, she watched the pair. Rafe got off to a rocky start, stumbling around the corral, but then he managed to stabilize his footing. Smiling, she made the dog come with her as she measured oats for Tano and her own two mares and one gelding.

When she was finished, Alexa returned to lean on the top rail of the corral to watch Rafe put Esperanza through changing gaits. She was struck by two things. First, there was a look of pure joy on his face. Second, he dug in the flat heels of his combat boots, wrapped the rope around his narrow hips and coaxed the exact gait out of the horse that barrel racers wanted.

Alexa whistled approvingly. "Hot dang, cowboy, y'all have that little lady eating out of your hand. I haven't been able to get her to transition like that from a walk to a trot to a canter. You're the man."

Rafe directed a wide smile over his left shoulder toward her voice. It singed Alexa's insides, and she felt the heat all the way to her toes.

Lordy, a scowling Rafe Eaglefeather had been a sight to behold. But when he smiled, he was pure devastation. Alexa felt knocked off-kilter. Then, for no reason at all, fear moved in, welding her to the top rail. Memories of Bobby swirled. She had failed him, and herself as well. What if her infusions, herbs and needles were no more than the hocus pocus Bobby's parents had claimed? Alexa shivered in spite of the sun.

Compadre set his paws on the middle rail of the corral and nudged Alexa's leg with his cold, wet nose, as if to say, *look at me. You doctored me back to health.*

Jumping down, she swept him into a hug. "I promise to give your new buddy my best, boy."

The collie licked her face.

But not even Compadre's vote of confidence could alleviate her concern.

CHAPTER THREE

"IF IT'S OKAY WITH YOU, I'd like to spend some time again tomorrow working with the mare," Rafe said as he and Alexa walked into the house for lunch.

"Fine with me. Like I said, Esperanza performed better to your commands."

"Really? Are you just saying that to pump up my ego?"

Alexa went over to the sink to wash her hands. "Like your ego needs pumping. You've got a healthy supply of machismo, Rafe."

"Are you saying I'm full of myself?"

Best not to reply to that, Alexa thought. "Is a cold ham-and-cheese sandwich okay with you?" she asked instead.

"Whatever. Food is food. You seem to be trying to change the subject. I thought you doctors always laid the truth on the line."

Alexa dried her hands and took down two plates from the cupboard. The truth was he looked damned sexy the way he casually propped one lean hip against her kitchen counter. He hadn't lost his military bearing, nor had he grown soft from lying around. His cheekbones and jaw were angular, but the small cleft in his chin kept his features from being too sharp.

"Your attitude sucks and you have a mile-high chip on your shoulder." That was one truth Alexa wasn't reluctant to share.

"That's calling a spade a spade." Rafe's lips thinned as he processed her blunt statement. Compadre woofed softly, gazing anxiously up at the man who'd stiffened beside him.

Alexa quickly prepared their lunch and set the plates on the table. "I put cut-up fruit on the side. Do you want a spoon or a fork for that?"

"Are you sure it's normal fruit, or some herbal crap like clover and dandelion leaves?"

"They're not fruits," Alexa said, snatching a whistling teakettle off the hot stove, "and that's the attitude I'm talking about. If I was treating you for infertility, I would use red clover buds and marigold flowers. But I honestly don't know what cures sarcasm."

She could see that Rafe tried to keep a straight face, but he couldn't quite manage. His laughter seemed to roll up from his belly.

"Great," Alexa shot back. "You've been hiding a sense of humor. Here. Sit down. These are apple slices and cantaloupe cubes from a melon I picked fresh this morning. You'll be happy to hear that today's tea is cinnamon," she added, pouring their mugs full of the spicy-scented brew.

Rafe took his seat as instructed and Alexa sensed how relaxed he felt.

She unfolded her napkin. "If you feel up to it, I thought maybe after lunch we could go for a ride."

"Where? Into town? I could buy some groceries."

Ignoring the dig at her food, Alexa said, "I meant go for a horseback ride. Sorry, I should have been more clear."

Rafe swallowed a bite of sandwich. "I need to be able to see to direct a horse." All levity had disappeared from his tone.

"I wouldn't have suggested a ride if I didn't think you could do it, Rafe. There are two or three easy park trails we can pick up just down the road. They're wide enough to ride two abreast. Plus, my horses are docile." Alexa could tell he was interested, but still debated the issue with himself.

"Docile, huh?" He gave a little snort. "Why bother saddling up, then? I might as well just sit in my room in the rocking chair?"

"Cute," she shot back. "Getting out helps sharpen other senses. I wouldn't send you out alone, Rafe, but people who have lost their eyesight still do sports—they ski, surf, play golf. Life changes with the loss of a limb or hearing or sight, but it doesn't have to end."

"Mine should have." The bitterness was back in his voice again. "Some of the guys in my unit who died that day had wives and kids. One had just got engaged."

Alexa didn't know what to say. He radiated guilt. She picked up her sandwich, but found she didn't have much of an appetite anymore.

"I was the man in charge," he added gloomily.

"Living here, safe and sound, you have no idea what it's like in the thick of war. No idea what it's like watching pals bleed to death because the enemy has you pinned down and there's not a damned thing you can do."

The apple slice Alexa had put in her mouth turned to sawdust. She knew exactly what it was like to lose a friend while she was in charge. Even now she could feel the shock of Bobby's hand going cold in hers. But she couldn't bring herself to share that with Rafe. One of them had to stay positive. "Only God is infallible," she said, almost to herself.

"Funny, my general said the same thing the day he stopped by my cot in the field hospital."

"What did you decide about the horseback ride?" Rising, Alexa collected their plates. "The weather's near perfect, and my horses need exercising."

Rafe unclenched his hand. "It's probably foolish, but you're right about the weather. I may as well take advantage of catching some rays. It won't be long until storms start rolling up from the gulf."

When they were ready to go, the dog headed toward the door with them. He stretched and yawned, then trotted up to nudge Rafe.

"You can't go this time, Compadre," Alexa said, stooping to rub his head.

"Why not?" Rafe asked.

"Park rules. Pets aren't permitted on park trails, and if campers bring dogs, they have to stay in camp and be leashed at all times. Wild animals do roam the park."

They headed out the door to the barn, Alexa's hand on his elbow to guide him.

"Oh, that makes me feel better about riding blind," Rafe grumbled.

Scoffing, Alexa gave his arm a friendly punch. "Not to worry, big guy. I'll save you from the raccoons, jackrabbits and skunks."

"Thanks," he drawled. "I'm more concerned about the coyotes, javelina and black bear."

"Hmm. I've ridden the lower trails almost daily for five years and have never seen a bear or javelina. You're more likely to come across a two-legged beast who's fleecing frightened illegals and sending them on their own through the park to hit the highway that leads to Alpine."

"They could be more dangerous," Rafe said thoughtfully.

"They're scum," Alexa burst out. "And they go to great lengths to avoid a law-abiding citizen who has a cell phone."

"Okay, you've sold me. I'm counting on you and your phone to protect me."

She smiled at that, but of course he couldn't see. "Do you want a mare to ride, or a gelding?" she asked. "I have two mares, Gigi and Willow. And a gelding, Loki."

"Are they all Andalusian?"

"Loki's an American quarter horse. The mares are no specific pedigree. How about you take Loki and I'll ride Willow today. I took Gigi out last time."

"I'd offer to help saddle up, but…" Rafe followed Alexa into the barn then stood awkwardly, acting out of place.

Alexa looked at his steel-toed combat boots, camouflage pants with cargo pockets and khaki T-shirt. She was about to suggest a clothes-buying spree when his cell phone rang.

Rafe dug the phone out of a side pocket and answered. "Hi, Sierra," he said after a moment. "Still can't resist checking up on me, huh?"

Alexa could hear a higher pitched voice coming over the line.

"I guess I'm doing okay," he said. "I helped train one of Alexa's horses to change gait on command. She and I are about to head out on a trail ride in the park."

He listened intently, all the while making faces, which drew a laugh out of Alexa.

"Yep, I said the same thing, Sierra." He nodded. "Alexa promised it'll be a cakewalk. What? She asked me not to call her Dr. Robinson. Sierra...there's no one out here to worry about proprieties. Okay, you worry, I'm going riding." He accepted the reins Alexa pressed into his right hand. "Gotta go," he told his sister. "I'll phone later and let you know how I did on the ride." Clicking off, he tucked the phone away and gave the saddle a shake to test the cinch.

"I wasn't eavesdropping on purpose," Alexa said. "Is your sister concerned about our lack of formality?"

"It's a Hispanic thing. Our mother was a stickler about using titles. A sign of respect, according to her."

"Ah, so your mother was Hispanic and your dad Native American?" Alexa inquired casually as she dropped down the fender and stirrup she had hooked over Willow's saddle horn while she cinched up the mare. "I didn't think about cultural taboos. If it bothers you, please go ahead and call me doctor."

"That's Sierra's hang-up. I take after my dad. We Native Americans are more laid-back. And Alexa is a pretty name. Unless you object, I'll continue using it."

Alexa felt the heat of a blush climb her neck. Shaking it off, she crooked a finger through both bridle rings and quickly led the horses out into a leaf-dappled, autumn after-noon. "Does anyone ever like their name? I hated mine. Kids at school called me Alex. They said my parents probably wanted a boy. I asked, but my mom insisted it's short for Alexandra, which was my dad's grand-mother's name. My first-grade teacher said it means to help, or defend. Maybe that's why I became a doctor," Alexa added, giving Rafe the barest assist into the saddle. He sat straight, although he seemed a tad uneasy.

"It's been a long time since I've tossed a leg over a horse," he said, as if reading Alexa's thoughts. "Feels good." He tested the stirrups for length and made sure Loki understood his rein signals.

Alexa swung up easily. "This pair of horses tends to want to gallop to the trail head. You may have to exert some pressure to hold Loki back to a trot."

"If Loki is sure-footed and the ground's fairly even, why don't we try a short gallop?" Just being on a horse seemed to give Rafe a confidence Alexa hadn't seen up to now.

"Your call," she said. "It's less than a half mile. And Willow can keep pace."

Rafe gathered the reins in his left hand. His grin reminded Alexa of an emerging sunbeam. Then he loosened his grip, and like a shot, horse and rider bolted. Alexa almost didn't catch up. And she was winded when she reached the tree line where Loki had slowed.

"Phew, are you all right?" She anxiously studied Rafe as she brought Willow back on her haunches less than a nose behind Loki's tail.

"Are you kidding?" Rafe said. "I love feeling the wind in my face. Honestly, I never expected to ride like the wind again."

Alexa couldn't see behind the shades he wore, but his voice sounded slightly choked and she wouldn't be at all surprised if Rafe had a tear in his eye. That humbled her.

"Quite a feat of trust," she said, emotional

herself. They entered the trail and rode under an arched canopy of old-growth trees. "I think loss of sight is the most difficult of all the five senses to lose."

"I agree," Rafe said. "A blind person is forced to rely on other people for so many things." He grew silent for a moment. "There's something else that bothers me. You know, for all the time we're spending together, I have no idea what you look like, Alexa. Please, can you describe yourself for me?"

She blushed, flustered by his question. Did he care how she looked, or was he just curious? Best to take his request with a little humor. "I could tell you I'm a dead ringer for Cameron Diaz."

"Who?"

"Come on. You weren't injured that long ago. Soldiers have zillions of movies at their disposal."

"You got me. Diaz is a babe. And you just made my point. Without sight I'm at your mercy."

"Well, who can describe themselves accurately?" she said hotly. "It's not easy."

He slowed Loki. "I guess you're right. I don't know what I'd say other than I'm six

foot tall and have black hair. It used to be
military short, but it's probably shaggy now."
He ran a hand through his thick, black curls,
then rested it back on the pommel. "This is
where you reel off your stats."

Before Alexa could say anything, a pair of
teacup-sized birds calling *jay, jay, jay* swept
out of a tree, startling the horses. Beside her,
Loki reared and came down stiff-legged.
Willow bolted, running the length of two foot-
ball fields before Alexa regained control. By
that point the trail had made a horseshoe turn
back toward the ranch and Alexa lost sight of
Rafe.

Guiding the mare around, she galloped
back to where a still-nervous Loki tossed
his head and crow-hopped first to one side
of the trail, then the other. But Rafe had him
in check. "What happened?" Rafe asked. "I
heard your horse take off running, and I didn't
know if she'd thrown you or not."

"Blue jays happened. When Loki was a colt,
one dive-bombed him. To this day their noisy
chatter is enough to send him off. I'm sorry. I
should have warned you. But you handled him
well, Rafe. Willow surprised me. Normally
she's unflappable."

Rafe's expression had darkened with concern.

"Shall we head on?" Alexa proposed. "This trail makes a big U back to within yards of where we started. We're about at the halfway point."

"What if you had been bucked off when the mare spooked?" Rafe demanded, his voice angry.

"I'm fine, Rafe," Alexa said soothingly.

Rafe sliced a hand through the air. "Don't patronize me. You could've gotten hurt bad, and what in the devil could I have done about it?"

"Stop borrowing trouble," Alexa snapped. "This trail is wide and flat. We'll have a nice, relaxing ride back to the ranch."

"I didn't see the jays—I didn't know what the hell happened," Rafe insisted. "For all I knew you could've been dragged off by a bear."

Rafe was overdramatizing and Alexa grew impatient. Then, she tried putting herself in his shoes. Yes, he was a big, strong man, a former soldier. But he was living in a dark, scary world. "Rafe, it really is rare to encounter any predators on these trails. Bear, mountain cats—they all live higher in the mountains. You were enjoying our ride. Don't worry about something that will likely never happen. Don't let it stop you from venturing out of your comfort zone."

"Are you really a shrink and Sierra didn't tell me?"

"Sorry if I sound preachy. I only wanted to reassure you. There's no need for you to act testy." Alexa touched Willow's flank and started off along the trail.

He caught up to her. "If I'm testy, maybe it's because you took away the pills that made me more tractable."

"Tractable?" Alexa raised her voice. "They made you catatonic. Tell me you don't like feeling…emotions," she said, groping for words. "Even if they're painful."

He rode along in silence for a minute, massaging the back of his neck with his free hand. "If honesty is what you want, then yes and no. I don't like…" It took Rafe a long time to search for the word he wanted. "Remembering."

Alexa could sympathize. For months or more after Bobby's death she would have loved to block the hurtful, pain-filled memories with a pill. How could she admit to Rafe that she still needed herb teas and mineral soaks to help her sleep most nights? But that was a burden she couldn't share. "Pills that turn you into a mechanical man aren't the answer. That kind of pain doesn't go away so easily, Rafe, it only gets buried deeper."

"Says you."

"Says me!"

"Is that why you chose to be an osteopath? Because MDs are too free handing out pills?"

"I became an osteopath because I graduated high school at fifteen and medical schools had age restrictions for entry."

"You graduated high school at fifteen?" Rafe whistled. "You must be a genius."

"*Gifted* is today's term." Alexa felt a pang of guilt. She hadn't been completely honest with Rafe. In fact, she had applied to medical school and been accepted, then...life changed.

They rode for a while in silence, then Alexa said, "Hey, we're breaking free of the trees. The ranch is a mile straight ahead, and Willow wants to run."

"Loki, too," Rafe said. "Let's go. Winner gets to choose what we eat for supper."

"You're on!" The ride would shake out the troubling memories gathering in Alexa's mind.

The horses ran neck and neck for half the distance, then Willow slowed and Loki's longer legs ate up the ground. Rafe won by ten lengths.

Alexa dismounted before Willow came to a complete stop. Although she was out of breath, Alexa laughed. "You won, Rafe. Fair and square. I hope you're not planning something high-fat like chicken-fried steak with biscuits smothered in gravy."

"Nope. A big, fat, juicy cheeseburger and French fries."

Alexa winced. "Almost as artery clogging. I probably have all we need on hand except for buns and enough oil to cook the fries." She opened the barn door, led Willow inside and started unsaddling her. Alexa was surprised and pleased when Rafe followed her, removing Loki's saddle with no help.

"Where's the brush?" he asked. "I'll brush both horses down if you want to go get the meal started."

"I was thinking, since I'd have to go buy buns and oil anyway, maybe we could eat in town. Rosita's Café does a good Tex-Mex burger. Or the tavern. I've never been there, but park rangers brag about their steak and fries." The idea grew on her as she passed Rafe a brush to use on Loki.

He made a few long strokes over the gelding's back before he answered. "I'm not ready to eat in public yet. I'm okay with passing on buns and fries this time. Winning the bet was no big deal. Racing was the kick for me. The adrenaline rush was nothing compared with bronc riding, but it felt good enough. I'd like to ride again tomorrow if you can make time."

"No problem. I ride most days. Tomorrow I'll ride Gigi. But I don't welch when I lose a bet. There's a general store at the park entrance. I can drive there and back in half an hour. Would you be okay finishing up here? I can bring Compadre out."

"I think I can manage. Show me which are their stalls. Oh, and are the oats easy to reach? Help me locate them, and a bucket to dip the oats." He seemed to hesitate a moment before speaking. "You know, it feels better than I ever imagined it would, doing chores again.

Alexa, I'm sorry I acted like such a butthead yesterday when you wanted me to help feed the animals."

"We all have days when things go wrong," she said, touching his arm.

"Yeah, but as you said," he muttered, "I started with a chip on my shoulder."

"More like a whole tree," she teased.

He laughed. "Okay. Rub it in."

"Rafe, today is a better day for you. But they're not all going to be good. Don't let the next down day send you back reaching for the pills that shut you off from the world."

"I'd like to try giving up all the crutches," he said, pausing in his brushing.

"Great. After supper we can look at possible alternatives to wean you completely off the meds."

Rafe nodded, and Alexa left to get Compadre. As a rule he'd whine to go with her in the pickup, but today he was content to stay with Rafe. Alexa found it interesting that the collie had been so devoted to Rafe in such a short period of time. Especially since Rafe continued to call him Dog, as if using a name made him feel too attached.

The man still had a long way to go.

COMPADRE MET ALEXA at the kitchen door with a happy bark on her return from the store. She set the buns and sunflower oil on the kitchen counter and went in search of Rafe.

She could hear him in the shower so she called his name and tapped loudly on his bedroom door. The water stopped and she heard him moving around.

"Everything went well in the barn," he called out, poking his head out the bathroom door. "Except I dropped a scoop of oats down the front of me. There's probably oat husks all over the bathroom floor."

Alexa was about to reply when Rafe walked into the bedroom, a towel wrapped around his hips, his hair wet, his chest muscles slick with water. She caught her breath. Rafe was stunning. The word *sexy* popped into Alexa's mind. She'd never dated much, and couldn't recall ever being struck mute merely by the sight of a man until now. Oh, she'd had a huge girlish crush on Bobby. But dear and sweet as he was, he'd never had a monogamous bone in his body. They were better being friends.

If she wasn't Rafe Eaglefeather's doctor… Alexa's fingers itched to explore that satiny bronze skin. She had to jerk her eyes away, and even then found herself stuttering when he spoke her name aloud again as if he wasn't sure she was still in the room.

"Uh, I didn't mean to interrupt your shower, but I brought you a surprise." She spun away from the sight of him to shake out the contents of the box and two bags she carried onto his bed. "The general store had just got in a new shipment of cowboy duds. I thought maybe you were sick of wearing your army stuff. If not…if I overstepped just say so," she continued nervously. "It's only a few pair of jeans, a couple of Western shirts and…gosh, I hope I guessed at the right size in boots. Leather tooled," she added.

Rafe crossed the room, crowding close to her.

Alexa felt heat emanating from his wide chest and fumbled with the silver-covered snaps on one of the three shirts.

"You bought me clothes?"

"Nothing fancy. Two shirts are blue, the third is gold. Jeans are—well, denim. Like I said, the boots are tooled brown leather. I'll run along and start the burgers if you want to try them on. Or not," she continued in a rush, dropping the shirt on the bed desperate to escape the heat from the bare, still damp body close to hers.

"Don't run off. Let me go put on a pair of shorts and I'll try them on now."

When Alexa said nothing, Rafe asked, "Will that embarrass you? I thought, uh, with the way you barged in here and jerked my covers off the other day and all…" He left the words hanging.

"Guilty as charged. If you must know, I was startled, but I was hardly going to admit it. At that point I felt I needed to flex my muscle."

"But you're a doctor. You must be used to dealing with male patients."

"Most men still tend to choose a male doctor in any field. And *you* didn't choose me, your sister did. But I should go start our burgers. You don't really need me to stay, do you?"

"No," Rafe hesitated. "I'm not real good at saying thank you. Other guys in the military got presents from their wives, or girlfriends, or moms. Sierra sent me things, but she's practical. Stuff like wet wipes and deodorant. But it's been ages since anyone bought me something for no special reason." He clutched a pair of jeans in both hands and shifted awkwardly.

"You're welcome, Rafe. I saw these and thought you might like to wear cowboy gear again. You are training my horse, after all. And remember, I'll exchange anything that doesn't fit. See you back in the kitchen for supper." She slipped out of the room, mentally kicking herself. Here she'd been beset with lustful thoughts while Rafe struggled with a dutiful thank you. She had to get a grip.

Some twenty minutes later he walked into the kitchen decked out in a new outfit. Alexa's heart tripped faster at the sight of him.

Compadre got up, sniffed Rafe's boots, then sat back and gave an excited bark.

"Wow, you look different," Alexa exclaimed. "But Compadre approves."

Rafe rubbed both hands down the front of a dark gold shirt that magnified the amber color of his eyes. "Been a long time since I've worn civvies. I don't look like a complete dude, do I?" he asked anxiously.

"You look like a rodeo cowboy to me." Alexa almost added, *a very hot rodeo cowboy*.

"Everything fit. The boots will take getting

used to. I've worn combat boots for the better part of nine years. I started thinking, though, it'll be good to discard the military trappings. My life was less complicated when I was a cowboy."

"You are what you are, Rafe, a cowboy turned military hero."

"I wasn't a hero," he said darkly. "A hero would've mowed down the enemy and saved all of his men."

Alexa couldn't let the comment pass. "I read your report and it disputes your version, Rafe. You shoved a corporal behind a boulder, and went out under fire to drag a private to safety. But, hey, let's find a new subject. One rule of alternative medicine is to keep meal-time conversations upbeat to aid digestion." Turning, she scooped the meat off the grill and deftly built two cheeseburgers. Then she flipped fries out of crackling oil onto folds of paper towels and dusted the hot potato strips with herbs and a little pepper.

Rafe took a seat in the chair he seemed to consider his spot. The dog immediately moved close and laid his muzzle across Rafe's thigh. "Mooch," he murmured, affectionately rubbing Compadre's silky ears. "I'll save you a bite of my cheeseburger, but you'll have to wait for it to cool." He bent his dark head toward the animal.

"He knows better than to beg for scraps at the table." Alexa chastened the dog with a look Compadre understood. Head down, the dog slunk off to lie in his usual spot near the door.

A soft touch herself, Alexa passed Rafe a cool piece of cooked hamburger. "Go put this in his bowl. I made it thinner for him."

Grinning, Rafe broke the meat into smaller pieces and carried it to the dog's dish. He was still smiling when he returned to the table.

His lazy smile made Alexa's skin tingle as she sat down across from him. People didn't call men beautiful, did they? But the truth was, Rafe was beautiful when he smiled. He had by far and away the most gorgeous eyes of any man Alexa had ever met. And his lashes were long and black and luscious.

He ate several bites and made delighted sounds before depositing the burger back on his plate. Then he dived into the still piping-hot fries, and after downing several, sighed. Cocking his head to one side, he asked, "Is something wrong with your burger, Alexa? Why aren't you eating?"

That's when she realized she still sat, chin propped in one hand, just watching him. "Honestly, I was sitting here wondering how many hearts you broke at every rodeo."

He smirked a purely male prideful smirk. "Is that question personal, or part of my medical evaluation?"

Alexa cleared her throat, saying primly, "Neither. Just a line I read somewhere that's guaranteed to be a great conversation starter."

"Oh."

From his nonverbal response, Alexa figured Rafe wasn't buying it. Best to direct the conversation along other lines. "Tell me what you liked best about riding in rodeos."

"The challenge," he said at once. "That, and the people there felt like family. I had Sierra, but she worked two jobs, and if she had any spare time she spent most of it with Doug."

"So they knew each other a long time." Alexa picked up her burger and bit into it.

"From first grade. Then when she was fifteen, at her *quinceañera*, Doug told our parents and his that he was going to graduate,

join the border patrol and marry Sierra."
Rafe slowly shook his head. "He had his life
mapped out at sixteen. Not me."

"Were you jealous of them?"

"Never. Probably more in awe of how both
knew exactly what they wanted in life."

"Rodeo, military—you didn't exactly
choose easy roads, Rafe."

"No, I suppose not."

As they neared the end of the meal, Rafe
told her about some of the tougher horses he'd
drawn to ride. "I taught myself to study each
twitch in a bronc's shoulder muscles. It sig-
naled which way he planned to buck. Turned
out to be a skill that helped on foot patrols
in Iraq. The guys all said I had magic, because I'd know before a seemingly innocent
shopkeeper pulled a weapon on us. Sight."
His voice sounded almost sorrowful. "Everything revolved around my ability to see and
prejudge a person's moves. Do you think I'll
ever get my sight back?" he abruptly asked.

"I won't lie, Rafe," she told him. "Your
military doctors found no ironclad reason for
your loss of vision. But they didn't project any
hope for reversing your condition. I doubt they
considered acupuncture. If you're interested,

I have some books on ancient Chinese techniques I can dig out and bone up on."

"Let me think about it," he said. "I'm not keen on doubling as a pin cushion."

"I understand," she murmured. He excused himself to go to bed as soon as he finished eating. Alexa hated that the turn of their conversation had clearly put a damper on what had otherwise been a really enjoyable day and evening. It was difficult for her to admit, but truthfully, she liked having Rafe Eaglefeather around.

CHAPTER FOUR

RAFE GOT READY FOR BED, but was too keyed up to sleep. His nerves were used to being brought down by two separate pills during the day, and another pill at night. Alexa allowed him only one tablet per day. Surprisingly, though, he felt more alert. More engaged. *Alive.* No, he cut himself off. He hadn't felt truly alive for months now, pills or no pills.

He had to acknowledge that Alexa Robinson and her smoky, sexy voice booted him in the butt the way nobody else had. He wanted to please her. Really, he wanted to *see* her. See her hair, her eyes, her expressions as she spoke.

Sitting in the rocker, petting Dog, Rafe mulled over the treatments Alexa had at her disposal beyond teas and herbs. He had no reason not to go to the mineral springs. Ego? Was he worried about his scars? Possibly. He didn't know how awful they looked. But Alexa must have already seen some of them.

That same reasoning ruled out any objections to massage. What about acupuncture? He straight-up got jitters picturing Alexa or anyone else poking him with a bunch of needles. But why? When he'd joined the service he'd watched grown men drop like rocks over a few pops with a vaccination needle gun. Not him. So why was he holding out?

If there was even the slimmest possibility that any of these treatments might restore his sight, he should have no objections.

Tomorrow he'd ask Alexa to take him on a trip to the hot springs, followed by a back massage, and then work his way up to the big daddy—acupuncture.

ALEXA RUBBED HER EYES and looked at the clock on her computer. Two-fifteen. She yawned and closed the books she'd been checking and cross-referencing online. Most of the information she'd read dealt with poultices for tired or overstrained eyes. Chinese herbalists agreed that there was no reversing congenital blindness. They weren't in such solid agreement when it came to other reasons for sight loss. Rafe's blindness was undefined. There was no evidence that he'd had a concussion or even blacked out, which left a huge gray area, the big mystery to medicine. Psychosomatic trauma of unspecified origin was the final diagnosis in his medical record.

How inconclusive. Why was the military so reluctant to attribute his condition to the ambush he'd been in? An attack where five in his troop had died. According to Sierra, two were Rafe's childhood friends.

Alexa surfed the Web awhile longer and ran across another possible reason for the evasive diagnosis. Money. Several soldiers had recently charged that they were being denied long-term VA benefits because military doctors hadn't diagnosed their disabilities as combat-related injuries, whereas doctors outside the military argued the opposite. Carefully worded notes in Rafe's chart could be aimed at cutting him from veteran disability payments. There was a pending lawsuit against the government concerning soldiers' rights to a second opinion.

Closing down her computer, Alexa felt torn. Should she continue to treat Rafe with nontraditional medicine? Maybe he should be at a VA facility. If driving proved too difficult for Sierra, maybe the two of them could split the travel. How many visits did Rafe need each month? Would going to the facility only frustrate him further? It was a dilemma.

She shut off the light and left her office. As she entered her bedroom, an image of Bobby materialized. He appeared before her with his old cocky smile, as if he wasn't a figment of her imagination. Rattled by the vision, she wondered if it was telling her she should send Rafe home when Sierra came to pick up his laundry? She hated to renege on an offer. And she'd said she would work with Rafe for thirty days.

It was a long time before she was able to shake Bobby's image.

The next morning she stood at the sink, cleaning and boxing fresh eggs she'd been out at dawn to gather, when a scraping sound drew her attention. Glancing around, she was surprised to see Rafe, dressed and striding down the hall with Compadre. That dog was such a traitor.

"You're up early." Alexa set down the egg

brush, and went to fill Compadre's food dish and water bowl.

"Is it early?" Rafe rubbed a hand over his chin, and Alexa noticed he hadn't shaved. "I forgot to set the alarm," he said. "The clock you put in my room has a glass face. I need to touch the hands to be able to tell what time it is."

"Of course. I'll remove the glass right after breakfast."

"No need. I've developed a kind of internal clock. Or maybe it's my stomach reminding me it's time to eat. Something smells good, by the way."

Alexa laughed. "I mixed up some oat bread and popped it in the bread machine before I went out to gather eggs. How does scrambled eggs, applesauce with a hint of rosemary, and hot oat bread sound?"

"Real good as a matter of fact. Sierra won't believe how much I've been eating. She complained I only picked at meals." He sounded surprised himself.

"Those pills you were on suppressed your appetite. Cutting back on them should get it back to normal. Also, you've been outside and moving around more. Exercise is a natural appetite stimulant. Do you want to work with Esperanza again today?"

"Sure. And you promised me another trail ride."

A bell dinged. Alexa opened the lid to the bread machine. She set a skillet on a hot burner and dumped in eggs she'd whisked while talking to Rafe.

"I did some thinking last night," Rafe said, leaning a hip against the counter, close to Alexa. He tucked his fingers under his belt in a casual move that drew Alexa's attention to his long legs and flat belly. She did her best not to drool.

"Thinking? About what?" she asked. Was it possible he'd come to the same conclusion she had—that he needed to give up his treatment with her and make an appointment with the VA? If so, she shouldn't have this sinking sensation in her stomach. She'd been a recluse for the better part of five years and it had suited her.

Rafe seemed to consider his words a minute. "I've been a real grinch about your suggestion of a soak in your mineral spring. I think I'd like to try it after today's ride. Mind you, I'm still leery of acupuncture, or massage therapy. Guys I knew who visited massage parlors went there for other…uh…services." Rafe's face scrunched and he fidgeted.

"Good grief! I'm a legitimate, licensed masseuse. In Houston where I practiced before moving here, women and men with stressful, high-powered careers came to me for my spa treatments. I had an eclectic clientele. I mix my own warm oils, and often combined massage with aromatherapy. You'd be surprised how those treatments can help ease tension and allow the body to relax and unwind."

Alexa had a fanciful vision of her hands spreading warm oil over Rafe's body and she shifted uneasily. She wondered if Rafe sensed her response because he suddenly turned and took a seat at the table.

"Before you gripe about the herbs in these scrambled eggs," she said, setting a steaming plate in front of Rafe, "let me tell you they're ordinary. Bits of fresh parsley and a hint of basil. Always good for whatever ails you."

Rafe merely grunted.

Alexa buttered thick slices of still warm bread. "I have a special treat for you today."

"Yeah?" He sounded dubious.

"Coffee." Happily, she set a steaming mug

in its usual spot near Rafe's right hand. "Instant, not brewed, and it's cut with chicory," she admitted, hovering over him.

"Will you sit down," he growled, sounding so grumpy that Compadre pawed at his leg and barked sharply several times.

"Well," Alexa huffed. Forcefully she yanked out her chair and plopped down. Had she actually been thinking it was nice to have him around? Moody jerk!

He picked up the mug. "I appreciate you going to all this extra effort."

Alexa knew stilted when she heard it. "By all means, don't strain yourself thanking me."

Rafe clammed up and turned his attention to his food.

As a result, they finished breakfast in total silence, until Alexa hopped up and cleared the table, including Rafe's unfinished coffee.

"Hey," he said, waving a hand over the empty spot.

He must have noticed how the air around them fairly crackled as Alexa slapped dishes into the dishwasher. She knew she was behaving badly, but she couldn't help herself.

He stood up. "Time to hightail it outta here,

Dog." Rafe beat a hasty retreat out the back door, letting the door slam shut behind him.

At the sink, miffed as she was, Alexa parted the window curtain and watched him saunter to the barn. She waved a cooling hand in front of her face. *Hoo-wee!* In his new boots, Rafe had the hip-rolling cowboy gait down pat—the one that made women all over Texas and elsewhere weak-kneed. How could she stay peeved at a man who had that effect on her?

By reminding herself Rafe was just her patient.

Bobby had been the only other patient who'd moved in with her during his illness. Which was like comparing apples and oranges. Outside of her friendship with Bobby, Alexa had precious little experience dealing with men and their temperaments.

She had to admit they had both acted passive-aggressively today. Not very adultlike. And here she was, once again letting herself feel too much for Rafe. She was eyeing him like a piece of chocolate. That had to change, Alexa vowed as she pulled on her gloves and went out to work with Tano.

She needed only half a corral. And Rafe wisely kept Esperanza well out of her way.

They had scant reason to talk as they both worked.

A pickup wheeled into the clearing about the time they finished up and were leading their horses back to the barn.

"Is that Sierra?" Rafe asked, pausing when he heard the vehicle brake to a stop. "Isn't she a week early?"

"It's Paul Goodman, one of the park rangers." Alexa waved as the man climbed from the cab bearing the park logo. "Halloo!" she hailed him. "I'll be with you in a jiffy."

WHAT RESONATED IMMEDIATELY with Rafe was the happy lilt to Alexa's voice as she greeted the man. Rafe's defenses went on full alert.

"We need to move these horses inside," Alexa told him. "Paul's gone to the back of his pickup. I see a cage, which means he's brought me another injured wild animal. It could spook the horses."

"What kind of animal?"

"I've no idea, but the scent is already making Esperanza edgy. Hurry, let's move them inside in case it's another mountain cat."

Rafe tightened his grip on the snorting

mare. He slid a forefinger through the halter ring and spoke soothingly.

Alexa opened both stall doors. Tano went straight to his water bucket. The mare whinnied and wouldn't stand still so Rafe could unhook her rope.

Stepping into the stall, Alexa handed Rafe a chunk of apple to entice Esperanza.

"We'll leave Compadre in the barn, too, until I see what Paul's brought," she said.

Rafe could volunteer to stay behind with the dog, but he was curious about this Paul Goodman guy. He didn't want to use the term jealous, but he had to admit there might be a little of that. He followed the sound of Alexa's boots crunching across the gravel.

"Paul, it's good to see you," Alexa said.

"It's been too long," came the smooth reply.

Rafe felt it the minute the other man entered his space. Sensed it the same way he knew Alexa had stripped off her gloves and tucked them in her back pocket. He didn't know if a quieter brush of flesh on flesh was a handshake or if their greeting was more kissy-face. Not knowing left Rafe grinding his back teeth, and he missed the pair's verbal exchange before Alexa said, "Paul, I'd like you to meet Rafe Eaglefeather. He's helping me train horses."

Next thing Rafe knew, Alexa took his elbow and guided his hand into Goodman's. It was awkward as hell, and both men muttered a passable "Pleased to meet'cha." Rafe attempted to disengage fast, but Alexa held his arm in a strong grip.

"Rafe's a former national bronc riding champion," she said. "More recently he's served with the army."

Paul hesitated too long. Rafe was acutely aware of the moment the guy realized Rafe couldn't see a lick.

"I'm Alexa's patient," Rafe snapped crossly. The SOB proceeded to pat Rafe's shoulder and ramp up the pity.

"Bummer, dude. But this is the first I've heard Alexa doctors two-legged critters." At once Goodman's tone turned flirtatious. "If I had known that, love," he said, addressing Alexa, "I'd have come a month ago to see if you had a potion for mendin' a broken heart." The ranger's attention was now totally on Alexa as he lowered his voice. "I s'pose you heard Jill left the area for the bright lights of the city over the summer."

"No," Alexa said, her surprise sounding genuine. "That's too bad, Paul. Now, what have got for me here?"

"First things first, darlin'. You just hafta come to the lodge Saturday night as my date for the rangers' fall charity dance."

Rafe had heard enough. He set off in what, if there was a God, would be the right direction to the house. Without the dog or Alexa to guide him, he might walk straight into the corral fence. Focused on his getaway, he couldn't hear if Alexa accepted Paul's invitation. No reason she shouldn't. She was a free agent.

The burning in his gut was his own problem, and something Rafe had no explanation for.

ALEXA FROWNED AFTER Rafe. She went so far as to skirt the back of the pickup for a clearer view of his zigzaggy march to the house. She wondered what he was using for reference points. He should have asked her to get Compadre. Taking off alone like that was reckless, and it bothered her. He could fall or smack into something.

"I brought you a pair of fox kits," Paul said. He took her hand and led her back to the pickup. "The ranger who found 'em figured a bobcat got Mama."

Relieved to see Rafe mount the steps to the back porch, Alexa finally peered into the cage. "What kind of injuries do they have?"

"None. They just need to be bottle-fed until they grow some."

"Don't you have someone skilled in being a surrogate to orphaned animals?"

"Shirl Scofield up in Marathon. Here's the real skinny, babe. Red Jones and some other guys bet me I couldn't get you to come to the dance with me.... Only you and I know you've always secretly had a crush on me," he concluded.

"Pardon?" Her mind back on Rafe, Alexa missed all but the last part of Paul's ludicrous statement. She gaped at him, open-mouthed.

"The kits gave me an excuse to come see you, as well as get the state to pay for my gas. I said to myself, one woman can mother these little guys as easily as another. After all, it's in a woman's genes. What say we meet at the lodge Saturday night, seven o'clock? I'll win enough off the guys to buy you dinner." Paul slid out the cage with the fox kits and strode off toward the small barn where she housed the wildlife.

Alexa couldn't believe his massive ego. She could easily see why Jill Harper, who clerked at the park general store, had ended their engagement. She'd like to kick Paul in the pants herself. Keeping step with him, she drawled sarcastically, "Gee, Paul. With kits to feed by hand three or four times a day, I can't possibly go off for an entire evening."

"Have your flunky feed 'em."

"Excuse me?" Alexa, who'd darted ahead to open the barn door, stopped dead.

"The blind dude. Have him feed the kits. Unless there's something more goin' on between you two besides him training your horses," Paul added snidely.

"Get lost, Paul," Alexa said icily. "I can't imagine what gave you the idea I treated you any differently than I treat the other rangers who drop off injured animals. A friendly wave or smile isn't a come-on. As for Major Eaglefeather, in my presence you will be respectful of him. Leave the foxes or take them to Mrs. Scofield. Either way, I'd like you to go now."

Paul shoved the cage at her, his eyes dark and angry. He opened his mouth to say something he would surely regret later, but Alexa angled her chin upward, and he apparently had second thoughts. Wise man. She watched him stalk back to his vehicle. What a bozo. His boss was a thirty-year veteran at this park and a true gentleman. He'd never tolerate Paul's bad behavior and Paul must know it.

Since she had baby foxes in her care, she needed to make a run to the store for canned milk. This time she wouldn't go to the park store, but to Study Butte. She wondered if she could talk Rafe into riding along and doing their trail ride another day.

She set the kits' cage well away from the hissing mountain cat. She'd have to ask Carl Dobbins, the ranger who'd brought in the cat, what his plans were for the healed animal. Alexa didn't want to let him out on the ranch where he could come back and stalk her goats, chickens or horses. A squirrel that someone had found with a broken leg was well enough to be let go, too. She didn't mind turning him out. In fact, she'd do it now.

After locking the small barn, she took the cage to the edge of the woods and held it up as high as she could against a tree limb. Then she went back to the horse barn to collect Compadre and they circled back to the house.

"Rafe," she called, hearing nothing when she walked in. Compadre made a beeline down the hall and nosed his way into Rafe's room, so Alexa followed.

"There you are," she said, concerned to find him sitting idle in the rocker in a dark room. Once again she went around opening his curtains.

"Would you mind if we cancel our afternoon ride? I need to run to the grocery store to pick up canned milk to feed those two baby foxes Paul brought."

"Go ahead," he said, giving a curt wave with one hand.

"Would you care to ride along?"

Rafe rocked faster. "Wouldn't your new boyfriend love that?"

"Paul left. And for the record, he's not my... anything. Not even a friend, which I might have considered him before today. He's an egotistical idiot."

"So, you're not going to the dance with him? I can have Sierra come take me to her place for the weekend, in case you…do a sleepover."

"What's with you men all presuming things? Did you not hear a word I said? Paul's an idiot. Do you want to ride to Study Butte, or not?" She pronounced the town's name the way locals did: *Stewdy Butte*.

"I apologize, Alexa. Study Butte, huh? I thought that town died."

"It has around three hundred residents. A few families struggle to keep basic businesses operating. The store should have what I need. Canned milk and baby food. The foxes are cute little stinkers. Gray fox, I'm pretty sure."

"Do you think the store carries swimsuits? I assume that's what you wear when you visit the hot springs."

"Well, I, uh…need to wear one now for sure," she said, feeling the heat rise to her cheeks. "Uh, if the store doesn't have a suit, I can cut off your oldest pair of long pants. I have a sewing machine. It won't take any time to zip in a hem."

"Maybe I'll let you do that. I know my cammo's fit. And they're comfortable."

"Mineral baths are all about comfort," Alexa said, glad to have dealt with that issue. "Then it's settled. I'll haul out my machine as soon as we return from the store."

"I REALLY LOVE THIS DRIVE through the park," Alexa said after they had been on the road about ten minutes. Before they'd set out, she had rolled down both windows in her pickup. Compadre, who usually had the passenger seat to himself, sat in the middle with his feet propped on Rafe's legs and his head poking out into the fresh air.

"It's a lot cooler here than at your ranch," Rafe noted. "Sierra said your place sits virtually by itself in a valley. I know it's peaceful. One of the worst things about being in the military is that you never have a minute alone. You're always with people. What about you, Alexa? I take it you don't mind not having neighbors?"

She drove with one arm propped on the window ledge, a casual hand on the steering wheel. "I grew up an only child," she said. "My dad was an oil man. A workaholic. He could retire, but he's branched out into wind and solar exploration. The folks still own the ranch, but they have a condo in Houston. When I was a sprout there were no close neighbors. Dad owned racehorses then. His vet lived on-site, as well as a trainer. I spent a lot of time tagging after them. It's where I developed an interest in animals and in medicine."

"Yet you didn't become a vet."

"Funny how stuff happens," Alexa said. She didn't really want to get into explaining the whole sordid tale about how she'd landed here. So, she launched into a new topic. "I don't know that I can help you regain your sight, Rafe. I want to be clear. Sierra is a bit of a steamroller, as I'm sure you know. She was so determined and so positive you'll respond to alternative healing methods that she convinced me to try."

"And now you doubt you can help me?"

Alexa vacillated, not wanting to take away any hope Rafe might cling to. Nor did she want to build false expectations.

"You're not saying anything," he murmured. "I take it the answer is no."

"In medicine you never say never, Rafe. There are always surprise outcomes. Instances that defy the odds."

"Miracles?" Rafe leaned his head back against the headrest and languidly stroked Compadre's spotted curls. The dog drew in his head from the window and licked Rafe's chin.

"Unexplained cures happen, yes, in rare cases. I've pored over your chart endlessly. No doctor who examined you gave clear-cut reasons for you not being able to see. There's no shrapnel in your brain. No obvious trauma to the eyes themselves or to the ocular nerves."

"The neurologist who examined me when I first came stateside thought maybe I'd been thrown against something when the first RPG exploded in our camp and that shook up or rattled my brain. I don't know. Much of that attack is a blur. What I do know came from doctors who treated other guys wounded that day." Rafe shifted in his seat and turned his head.

That caused Alexa to skip to another

subject, even though she would have loved to ask if he had gained any specific memories from his flashbacks. She was afraid those memories might be too painful. "We've arrived, Rafe. We're at the thriving metropolis of Study Butte. I was close when I said three hundred residents. The sign as you enter town has been scratched out a few times, but now reads two hundred seventy-one."

Rafe wrinkled his brow. "I'm trying to remember what they mined here. Not silver."

"Cinnabar," Alexa supplied, pulling to a stop in front of an adobe building that still had an ancient hitching post out front. "The store owner told me most outsiders who come here these days are rock hounds. They comb the mine tailings for cinnabar or other colorful pieces that can be made into jewelry. Do you want to come in the store or wait in the pickup? Compadre has to stay."

The collie hung his head at those words, but burrowed against Rafe.

"Did you bring Dog's leash?" Rafe felt around in his fur for a collar. "I could get out and stretch my legs with him. Is there a sidewalk, or are we in danger of being run over by a car?"

Alexa had gotten out of the cab and was digging under the seat. "I always carry a spare leash. Here." She snapped it on the dog and tucked the leather wrist loop into Rafe's hand. "There's no sidewalk, but if two vehicles a day drive down this street it's probably a traffic jam. Just stick close to the side and you should be fine."

Rafe laughed as he took a firmer grip on the leash and opened his door.

Alexa's stomach gave a funny little jiggle. The man's laughter turned her inside out. And the change it made to his features squeezed her heart. He smiled so rarely that a laugh was a treasure. If she never helped him in any other way, her mission from now on was to make him laugh more often.

Alexa entered the small store and passed the time of day with the owner as she filled her basket with the items she'd come for. She also bought yams that looked fresh. "They're grown locally," the owner said. And when she rang up the canned milk and baby food, the woman asked if Alexa had gotten married.

"Oh, no. I acquired a pair of fox babies who lost their mother."

The jovial Hispanic woman winked. "I

noticed the handsome hombre you're with today."

Alexa knew she turned red. "He's just a friend," she said, pocketing her change. On leaving the store, she realized she'd specifically not identified Rafe as her patient to Paul or this woman. Truth was, he felt more like a friend. How wise was that? she mused, fumbling the keys as she called to Rafe. She climbed in the vehicle and shook off the negative thoughts. The day was too lovely to spoil with old worries.

Back at the ranch, Alexa hummed while she unpacked her purchases. "Okay, go get the pants you want cut off," she told Rafe. "The sewing machine is in my office. It'll only take a minute to set it up and thread it with khaki thread."

"Do they need hemming? Can't we whack them off and leave them ragged?"

"Threads might unravel and clog the spring. It's better environmentally to keep the water as pure as possible. So no sunscreen or other skin products, please."

Rafe shrugged. "These days I use the least amount of stuff like that as I can. In Iraq, even dark as my skin is, I slathered on sunblock. In the hospital, nurses gave me vitamin E cream to rub on my wounds so they wouldn't scar. I ran out, so I should prepare you for how bad they must look. One bullet tore out a lot of muscle and skin."

"I saw them already, if you recall. They weren't all that shocking, Rafe. Anyway, for me, the human body is like a canvas is to an artist," she quipped.

Rafe looked as if he wasn't sure what she meant by that, but all he said was, "I'll go find those pants."

Alexa cut the pants off above the cargo pockets. She hemmed them and passed them back to Rafe. "Go change. I'll grab towels and meet you outside. Compadre has to stay here. My grandfather built an enclosed gazebo around the spring to keep wild animals out and it gets a bit like a steam bath inside. The minerals help cleanse the pores. Good for people, not so good for dogs."

"Lead on," Rafe said when he joined her on the porch a few minutes later.

They hiked the short distance to the isolated spring in silence. As they walked, Alexa cast sidelong glances at Rafe, who in spite of his scars was plenty ripped.

"How hot is the water?" he asked as they entered the enclosure. He must have been able to feel the steam and hear the bubbling water.

"The spring first comes out of the ground at around a hundred forty degrees Fahrenheit. It's artesian fed. This pool my grandfather carved out is gravity fed and naturally cooled to approximately ninety-eight."

She stepped in and reached for Rafe's hand.

"Oh, there's a seat." He sighed as he sank slowly down until the water came up to his pecs. "It must be up to your neck," he said, turning to Alexa.

"My shoulders. I'm not much shorter than you, Rafe."

"And you look like Cameron Diaz," he murmured with a smile.

"Or Gwyneth Paltrow," she teased. "What if I look like Rosie the Riveter?"

"I probably wouldn't care. To me you're the woman who jump-started my life, first by letting me help you train horses and then taking me riding. And now you're allowing me to share this slice of heaven." He leaned back and closed his eyes.

"I told you it was nice, ye of little faith. After a soak we'll go back to my office and I'll give you a therapeutic deep-tissue back massage. If you like it, one day soon I'll set you up with an herb body wrap."

"Don't be getting too fancy," he warned.

RAFE DIDN'T OBJECT WHEN Alexa dribbled warm scented oil over his back. And he practically purred like a kitten when she kneaded his shoulders.

"I thought you'd make me smell all flowery," he grumbled. "What is that scent?" Rafe hoped if he kept talking, he could ignore the sensations of Alexa's fingers working magic on his back. His mind envisioned her touching him all over and he could barely lie still.

"This oil is a blend of bergamot and patchouli. Both potent manly scents."

Great, Rafe thought. If he felt any more potently masculine, they'd both be in trouble.

"No kidding," was all he said. But despite his heightened awareness of Alexa's touch, Rafe was almost asleep by the time she finished and told him to sit up. He did and shrugged both shoulders. "I suppose now that you've got me all rag-doll relaxed, you'll talk me into acupuncture."

Alexa turned aside to store her oils. "Rafe, I want you to progress at your own pace. You tell me when you're ready."

Rafe already missed the touch of her soothing hands, but a man knew when he'd had enough.

SIERRA DROPPED BY MONDAY to pick up Rafe's laundry, sticking to her excuse to check up on him. Her brother was giving Esperanza a workout and Alexa watched their exchange from the barn.

"Rafe, look at you," Sierra cried, obviously delighted. "Does this mean your sight's coming back?"

"Not so far," he told her. "What I'm doing with the mare comes totally from memory."

"There's no progress?" She sounded disappointed. "I pray every day. Oh, by the way, Rafe, earlier this week a counselor from the VA called to speak with you. Ms. Holmes. I explained you're seeing Dr. Robinson, our local healer. She didn't sound pleased. Do you think I made a mistake bringing you here? I don't want to get you in trouble with the VA, Rafe."

"You did right, Sierra. I never expected to, but I'm feeling better each day."

"If you're sure…." His sister's uncertainty hung between them even as she set down his bundle of dirty clothes and hugged him goodbye.

Alexa walked out of the barn and waved goodbye, all the while wondering if Sierra's doubts were valid. And yet after their visit to the hot springs and the massage therapy that followed, she could sense the protective layers peeling away from Rafe and found he was engaging more in the world around him.

Still, she worried she was growing too attached. Maybe Rafe hadn't come to her expecting a cure, but she was pretty certain he believed it possible now. He pressed her for success stories involving alternative treatments, and he started to sound hopeful that they would restore his sight.

But what if she made him worse? That worry caused Alexa sleepless nights.

Thursday, after supper, seemingly out of the blue, Rafe said, "I'm ready to take the next step with those needles, Alexa."

"You mean acupuncture?" Her heart skipped. If the oldest remedy in her bag of tricks didn't help Rafe, there would be no reason for him to remain at her ranch. She'd grown used to having him around and the thought of saying goodbye hurt. Why, oh why had she agreed to treat him?

She told Rafe she wasn't sure he was ready yet but knew she couldn't put him off forever.

CHAPTER FIVE

FRIDAY MORNING AFTER breakfast Rafe told Alexa he was determined to try acupuncture. He said he had more energy than at any time since his injury. He felt healthier. It was time to find out if his eyes could be stimulated to see again.

Alexa felt a wave of panic as she loaded the dishwasher. Luckily Rafe didn't seem to detect her tension.

"You've answered a million of my questions," he went on, his enthusiasm evident. "I understand it's an art of healing discovered twenty-five hundred years ago by the Chinese. I get that there's no modern medical rationale, and that a lot of doctors say it's no better than a placebo. But I'm ready to give it a whirl. I want to start today."

"To…day?" Alexa's voice cracked. "Why the rush?" She straightened.

"During yesterday's hot-rock massage you

said my yin and yang are out of whack. If you believe what you said about Qi being the vital flow of a person's energy, then why are you reluctant to try to unblock mine?"

Lordy, the man had been paying attention.

Alexa reached for his hand. "Rafe, I c-care about you," she stammered. "I swear I only want what's best for you. But…in all of my books on acupuncture I've found no proven treatment to reverse blindness."

Rafe turned his hand over and brought hers to his mouth. The searing heat from his lips sent fiery shocks up her arm. "I know you care, Alexa. That comes through in everything you've done for me, even when I was a real pain in the ass those first few days. I never thought I'd ever care about anything again, but *you* brought about a change."

He ran his thumb over her fingers and the heat in Alexa grew.

"The truth is," Rafe said simply, "I'm no longer content to imagine what you look like. I want to *see* you, Alexa."

Her heart threatened to leap out of her chest. By sheer will she forced herself to calm down. "Rafe…I'm flattered." She snatched back her hand. She wanted to do the right thing here—to set the right tone. "I realize that because this is my home and not a regular clinic, you might view our therapy as less professional than the treatment you'd get with the VA."

"Bull pucky," Rafe broke in. "I've made more progress here than all those months with the military."

He was so close to her, Alexa could feel his heat. She could barely find the words to speak. "You're, ah, certainly more…alert."

He reached for her and slid his hands up and down her upper arms. "Then explain your problem."

She turned her head away from his handsome face in order to pull her thoughts together. "Holistic medicine is as serious as traditional medicine. As my patient, Rafe, you need to be fully committed—you need to totally want a cure for yourself."

He sobered. "I couldn't be any more committed, Alexa."

His words blew away the last of her arguments. "All right," she managed to say as she wedged a bigger space between them. "I'll set up for your first treatment right after I feed the animals."

The minute Rafe dropped his hands, Alexa grabbed her gloves and streaked out the back door. Not until she stepped inside the cool wild-animal barn did she stop cursing her inability to resist Rafe.

But, true to her word, once she'd finished her chores and had washed up, she put a new cover on the massage table in her office.

"Take off your shirt and lie face up," she told Rafe when she'd set up everything she needed. At least she'd regained her clinical objectivity.

He stripped off his blue shirt and stretched out on his back as she'd directed.

The sight of him shirtless caused a now familiar tightness in Alexa's belly. As she'd done every day since they'd first started massage, she did her best to ignore the feeling. "I'll work mainly on meridians around your head and shoulders today with sterile, disposable needles. Each is no thicker than a hair." She pulled on plastic gloves and swabbed the areas with alcohol.

"I can't believe I'm doing this," he murmured.

Alexa had torn open a pack of needles. "We can stop right here."

"No. Go on. You said there are rarely complications." There was only a hint of curiosity in the statement but no reservation.

"True. You may feel a little prick, but it shouldn't hurt." She'd done the procedure scores of times, but still, this was Rafe. Alexa held her breath as she inserted the first needle at the midpoint between his eyes. He didn't bat a lash. Slowly, ever so slowly, she continued around his hairline and behind his ears.

He was fully relaxed by the time she reached the trapezius muscles that ran from his neck to his shoulder. Alexa went back and spun the strategic needles gently. Then she began removing them. The whole process took twenty minutes.

"Your first session is over," she said, taking off her gloves and tossing them and the needles in a special waste receptacle. "It's not uncommon to be dizzy, so sit up slowly."

"That's it?" Rafe sat up, moved his head side to side and blinked several times.

"How do you feel?"

"I feel nothing. A while ago I experienced a brief, deep ache at the back of my head." He held out his hands and frowned. "Everything's still black."

"Success isn't instantaneous, Rafe. You'll need more sessions—once or twice a week."

"Twice a week," he said, climbing off the table. "I want the fast track."

She handed him his shirt. "We'll try another session Tuesday."

Plainly restless and frustrated, Rafe retreated to his room.

In a way, Alexa was relieved. But she couldn't help feeling another dip in her confidence as an effective healer.

Over the weekend it was obvious Rafe was disappointed. Except for meals and the hours he spent with Esperanza, he kept to his room.

She'd tried to make him be realistic in his expectations, Alexa thought, but maybe he was still putting too much store in the procedure. And what if all the teachers who'd called her gifted had been dead wrong?

TUESDAY, RAFE TRACKED Alexa down in the wild-animal barn when she didn't show up at her office for his second treatment. The dog, who didn't like this barn, nervously tried to nudge him outside again. "Alexa, did you forget it's Tuesday?"

"How did you know where to find me?" She sounded peeved.

"Dog found you. What's with you? Don't you want to treat me?"

"What a thing to ask. Of course I do. But I also want you to be realistic. Acupuncture is no guarantee you'll get your sight back."

He heard her return the fox babies to their cage and drop the bottles she used to feed them into a basket.

Alexa brushed past him. "Be sure to latch the door. I'll meet you in the office after I put these in the dishwasher, and then scrub up."

Their second session was similar to the first, except Alexa added electric stimulation to some of the needles. Rafe fell asleep during the procedure.

Alexa had to shake him awake after she removed the needles.

Yawning, he sat up more slowly than before, then he stretched out his hands before him. But this time Rafe saw more than darkness.

"Alexa." His voice rose excitedly. "It's working. The acupuncture." He slid off the table and hugged her hard. "I can distinguish

shapes," he shouted. "They're murky, but…"
Finding her face, he planted a kiss squarely
on her lips.

Rafe felt her rise up on tiptoes and lose herself in the kiss. She clasped his waist, and his
bare skin grew hot at her touch. Gripping him
tighter, she pressed closer until their thighs
met.

Rafe ground his pelvis against hers. Then
he tilted his head and slanted his lips over her
mouth, deepening the kiss. Breathing heavily,
he lifted his head a fraction. "I can see your
outline, Alexa."

He ran his thumbs over her cheekbones,
confident from her response that she was as
aroused as he was. He would tell her exactly
how he felt. "It's the first step. When I can
see all of you, I'm taking you skinny dipping
in the hot springs. I'll carry you every step
of the way. Alexa, do you have any idea how
many nights I dream of that? Every one since
our first trip there."

Even as Rafe lifted her feet off the floor and
spun around, he could feel her tense. "Rafe,
stop!" She wiggled until he let her slide down
the length of him and her feet landed on the
tile floor.

She broke free and he forced himself not to reach out for her again. "Rafe, I'm happy for you. Distinguishing shadows is fantastic. But we can't get carried away. I thought I made it clear on Friday that everything we're doing is to help you get well again—it's professional therapy. Rafe, I'm a doctor. You're my patient."

He laughed, bent and kissed her again.

"I mean it, Rafe. This is…not ethical." Her voice was not that of a woman who wanted to be kissed.

He recoiled as if she'd slapped him. *He was nothing but a patient to her?* Stunned after experiencing such joy, he grabbed up his shirt and shrugged it on. The shadowy outlines of the massage table, a bookcase and shelves with rows of bottles floated before him in a black mist. The truth hit him like a brick. Why would a woman like Alexa ever want to saddle herself with a guy like him? Someone who couldn't even distinguish what she looked like? He knew she had a narrow face. And heavenly soft lips. But that was it. He wasn't a whole man, and she'd been trying to break it to him over the last week that he might never be completely healed.

Her hand rested on his bare arm but he pulled away.

"Don't look like that, Rafe." Her voice was calmer now. "The last thing I want is to hurt your feelings. But I'm right about this. You know I am. A doctor has to tread a fine line. It's easy to fall for a patient. Especially when we're living here together. It's practically inevitable. But I can't ever forget that your sister placed her trust in my ability to heal you, Rafe, not to seduce you."

He was already feeling like a complete fool. No use hanging around just to be hurt more.

"Forget it," he said gruffly. "You made your point. Friday's my next session, right?"

Taking extra care not to brush against her, Rafe fled the office for the sanctuary of his room.

ALEXA HAD SOME awkward moments with Rafe the next few days as they both tried to avoid each other. Late Thursday, a cold wind blew down from the north and they agreed to shorten Tano and Esperanza's training session. On the way back to the house from the barn, Rafe shivered and unrolled his shirt-sleeves.

"Where's your jacket?" Alexa asked.

"I have a sweatshirt back in the house. But this wind will be gone tomorrow."

"Not according to the weatherman. I'm glad I picked what remained of the beans and brought in the last squash. There was frost on the roof of the chicken coop this morning. The almanac says we're in for an early winter."

"Winters here are nothing compared to what we had in the mountains of Afghanistan." He appeared lost in thought as they walked side by side. Alexa didn't want Rafe dwelling on the war. He hadn't had a flashback since the one in the barn when he'd first arrived. Then it hit her. His month's stay was almost up.

"I'll skip supper tonight and turn in early," he said as she opened the back door. "Can we schedule my acupuncture treatment for first thing tomorrow morning?"

A whistling gust of wind momentarily diverted their attention. Compadre barked, nosed open the door and slunk inside. "Skipping meals isn't good for you," Alexa said. "Before we went to the corral I put on a Crock-Pot of chicken noodle soup. If you stick around, I'll light a fire in the living room. We can eat hot soup and bread in there."

He shrugged offhandedly, and Alexa knew if he left he'd just sit and brood in his room.

"I don't hear any noise from you in the evening," he said as they went to the living room. "You must not watch TV like Sierra and her family do."

"I've never been big on TV. World news I pick up online. Most nights I read. And I have a CD player in my bedroom. I can bring it out if you'd like to listen to music."

He rubbed the back of his neck. A nervous gesture? Or was he feeling tense? After Tuesday, they'd both steered clear of any mention of another massage.

"Sure," he finally said. "What kind of music? In the field, guys played everything from classical to rap. Raised here, my favorite is country-western."

"Mine, too."

"Do you have any Rascal Flatts, George Strait or Brooks and Dunn?"

"All three." She made an extra effort to sound upbeat. "I'll go start a fire. You grab a spot on the sofa. I'll bring my CD player and then dish up our soup."

"That sounds like a big bother for you."

"It's no trouble. And to be honest, I get tired of my own company. In case you hadn't noticed, even my dog has deserted me since you moved in."

"Sorry." Rafe sounded like he meant it. "Dog sticks to me like glue, but danged if I know why."

"He bonded that first night," Alexa said, taking a long match from a tin box that sat on the mantel. "At least he figured you to be a good friend." She knelt to fan the small flame.

"If he could talk I'd tell him I'm a lousy gamble."

She glanced up sharply. "How so?"

"I let my buddies die in an ambush I should have seen coming."

"Nobody sees an *ambush* coming, Rafe. That's the nature of the beast. Anyway, dogs are excellent judges of character."

Rafe grunted and leaned toward the fire, stretching his big hands toward the struggling flame.

Looking at him, seeing the rawness of his self-blame, Alexa ached for him. "Soak up the warmth. I'll be right back."

She returned with the CD player and put on her favorite songs by George Strait, hoping the music would help shake Rafe out of his despondent mood.

He remained uncommunicative throughout their meal. As Alexa collected his empty bowl, their fingertips tangled. He held on to her hand longer than necessary. "Oops," she said. But he'd already pulled back. "The CD's ended." That was pretty obvious, she thought, but she had to say something. "Give me a minute to rinse these, and I'll tell you the other album titles. You choose what to play next."

Rafe shifted his large frame in the couch. "I think I'll hit the sack. I'm sure you have better things to do than babysit a blind guy."

"That doesn't say much about me, Rafe."

He sat in stony silence for a long minute. When she finally headed for the kitchen, he said, "The fire is nice. If you'll hand me another CD, I'll put it on while you tidy the kitchen."

She dropped an empty case in his lap, along with a Keith Urban CD. If Rafe didn't like Keith—tough.

As she rinsed bowls and stomped around

the kitchen, Alexa admitted she was a tad bitchy herself. She hated the way she'd snapped at him Tuesday and she knew she was responsible for the tension that had been between them since then. She couldn't give Rafe the intimacy he seemed to want, yet she liked having him just sitting near her, on her terms.

She returned to find Rafe leaning back on the couch cushion, eyes closed, one hand stroking Compadre's head in time to Keith's guitar. Alexa stood a moment, soaking in the sight, afraid to make a noise and have him get up and walk out of her life this chilly night.

He turned his head. "I'm not asleep."

She scooted past him, curled up in the recliner, and hurriedly opened the book she'd been reading. "I tried to be quiet."

"My hearing's not a problem. There's nothing wrong with any part of my body except for my eyes."

Alexa wasn't about to touch that remark. She started to read, struggling to concentrate on the words.

"Is that a book you have? I see a black blob between your hands."

"Yes, it's a book." She marked the spot with

her finger. "Rafe, there's not one shred of data to support the progress you made with your last treatment. If you continue to improve you'll make history."

"I'm afraid to wish for a full recovery. Afraid I'll jinx my chances."

"That's too superstitious for me. Oh, I know some people think holistic medicine is mumbo jumbo. But so little is really known about the human mind. Did you know that two of the doctors who examined you said your subconscious could be suppressing your vision?"

"That's like saying I don't want to see. What a load of crap."

Alexa flinched. "A psychosomatic illness can manifest itself in powerful ways."

"I'm not wasting my time seeing the VA shrinks if that's what you're suggesting, and that's final." Rafe stuck out his jaw pugnaciously.

"Is that what someone recommended? That you see a psychiatrist?"

"Colonel Baker, the officer who signed my discharge, said it was the next step. I told him, I told Sierra, and I'll tell you. It's off the table. Nobody's poking around inside my head."

"I poked needles in your head, Rafe."

"That's different. You don't dig in my past. Don't ask what kind of thrill I got out of riding bucking horses, or how I felt shooting at enemies. If you had, I'd have been out of here before you could snap your fingers."

Alexa had nothing to say to that. She wasn't a psychiatrist. And she'd been lousy at psychoanalyzing herself.

Getting up, she put another log on the fire. "I wonder how long this cold snap will last."

"Depends on the jet streams. If memory serves, they're erratic as well this time of year. How's your wood supply?"

"I have plenty. My grandfather ordered five cord every year from a local man who split and stacked the wood in the shed. Now his son runs the business."

"Good, because I'm not sure I can see well enough to split wood."

Alexa eyed him over the pair of reading glasses she'd put on. "I have a feeling you can do anything you set your mind to, Rafe."

Compadre turned and set a paw on Rafe's knee, making a guttural sound.

"See, Compadre agrees," Alexa said, laughing.

Rafe smiled and let his head loll back. For a time the house was silent except for an occasional crackle and thump when a log dropped. Or when the wind rattled the windows.

"What are you reading?" Rafe inquired sleepily.

"A collection of short stories by Mark Twain," Alexa told him.

"Huh. I remember Sierra reading *Huckleberry Finn* to me ages ago."

"These are some of his lesser-known works, but they're all entertaining as only Twain can be. Would you like me to read out loud, Rafe?"

"I'm not a child, Alexa," he said sharply. "Don't try to treat me like one."

The man certainly could be prickly, Alexa thought. "No, you're definitely not a child. But…I'm trying to picture you as a little boy." She set her book aside and removed her glasses to study him. "Were you rough and tumble? I can see you climbing trees and chasing little girls with tarantulas."

His short laugh was little more than a rumble in his chest. "Childhood was so long ago it almost feels as if I never was a kid. I definitely recall chasing girls, but not with tarantulas." This time his laugh was that of a man who had no trouble catching the women he chased.

"I get your drift. You were a young Casanova. Did you live in Terlingua? In the town, I mean?"

"Calling Terlingua a town is a stretch. It's the back of beyond. Its biggest claim to fame is that once a year chili-heads descend in droves for a national chili cook-off. Any permanent population to speak of live on outlying ranches and farms. Apache and Comanche had all that land to themselves until Mexican shepherds moved in and settled. The two cultures learned to coexist, which explains my mixed lineage."

"That's a rich history, Rafe. So, was your father Apache or Comanche?"

"The Eaglefeathers are Comanche. According to Dad that's why we're good with horses. He could never afford to raise them, with the cost of feed, so he had a sheep farm. But he kept one horse that he hand-trained for calf roping." Rafe's hand stilled on the dog's head, and the look on his face told Alexa he was cruising through fond memories.

"I take it those were some good times."

He nodded. "All week my folks worked their butts off with the sheep. Sierra and I went to school. But Saturdays were special. Dad loaded King in a rickety horse trailer and hooked it up to his ancient pickup. It was so old that I wonder how it made it to area rodeos. Dad always won. He could've been a world champion calf roper, but with a family of four, he never could scrape up the entry fee for big-purse rodeos. But that's another story. He and I would get home late. My mother always prepared a victory supper. Neighbors rolled in from miles around. It's no wonder we were poor. My mom was a great cook, and her dishes had disappeared by midnight. All the kids fell asleep to the sound of laughter and Spanish guitar music."

Alexa felt his joy. "You have great memories, Rafe. What a shame your parents died so young. Sierra's kids will miss all the love their grandparents could have given them. Kids thrive on love, not money."

"Yeah. I have more money put away now than my dad made in his entire life. And Sierra and Doug own a nice ranch-style home, and they're adding on a bedroom and another bath. The house we grew up in would probably fit in Sierra's living room, and she thinks it's too small."

"I take it the military has been good to you."

Rafe sat forward, braced his forearms on his knees and made what looked like a grimace. Alexa thought that was going to be the end of their conversation.

"Good and bad," he muttered after a long silence.

"Of course. It's not good that you were injured. And you lost your two best friends from your old home town in the same day."

Rafe's head jerked up. "Who told you about Joey and Mike?"

"You did, in a way. You know, it might help to talk about your friends."

"No. No amount of talk will bring Mike and Joey back to their families. And it won't bring back my eyesight. I thought I was clear, Alexa. Stay out of my head. You and the VA." He vaulted up, displacing the snoozing Compadre.

"For heaven's sake, Rafe, stop jumping to conclusions. All my questions tonight were out of interest. I don't have enough training to analyze you. I know you've had two flashbacks since you came here. And sometimes I hear you pacing around at night. But beyond the relaxation techniques I haven't a clue how to treat post-traumatic stress." She stood up and walked over to shut off the music. "You're quite welcome to your ghosts, Rafe. For your information, all God's children have got plenty of their own."

"The military docs asked me how I felt losing half my patrol. They asked me how I felt letting my two best friends go on point together. How the hell do they or anyone else think I felt?"

"Rafe, you don't need to talk about this. Do you want some pie and a glass of milk before you go to bed?" Alexa knew he was a bundle of nerves. It didn't take a genius to know it wouldn't be a good idea for him to go to bed without first calming down.

"We have pie? What kind? Where did it come from?"

"Pumpkin. Well, squash. I made it last night."

"Ah. So who else was up pacing around last night?"

"My mother called. She gives me insomnia."

Rafe followed her to the kitchen. "Really? Why?"

Alexa huffed out a tight breath. "She spent the first half of my life too busy with charities to pay me any attention. Then when I hit twenty, she decided she needed to control my life."

"From Houston?"

"Since I moved here, yes. She thinks I can drop everything here and fly home whenever she calls. Or that they can pop in unannounced to check up on me."

"Ouch. And you're how old?"

"Thirty," she snapped. "Weren't we going to have dessert?"

"Hey—I just thought of something. I've been here, what? Close to a month? And in all that time you've never served dessert."

"I am now. So enjoy it." Alexa got out two plates and took the pie from the fridge.

"Yeah, well I'm thinking squash is pretty normal for you." He sniffed the slice of pie she handed him. "You didn't put any of those weird herbs in here, did you?"

"Oh, for Pete's sake! All this because I put rose hips and marigold seeds in a couple of salads?"

"And dandelion leaves in place of lettuce."

"Mixed with romaine." She sat down and ate a bite of her pie. "If you don't like the meals here, then I guess you'll be anxious to go home with Sierra next week. A week from tomorrow, actually."

Rafe's fork stopped halfway to his mouth. "What makes you think that?"

"I don't feed you dessert. I make funny salads. I'm guessing Sierra cooks a lot like your mother did. Tonight you all but drooled when you spoke of her food."

"My mom made great *albondigas* soup, homemade tamales and chile rellenos. And my favorite dessert is probably a toss-up between churros and *almendrado*." He polished off the final bite of pie. "I may seriously have to add squash pie to my list."

"Flattery gets you nowhere, bub. Supper tomorrow night is still going to be vegetable kebabs. What's *almendrado?* I've never heard of it and I've eaten in tons of Mexican restaurants."

"I can't tell you what's in it. My mom didn't use a recipe. She started out with a pan of white, pink and green puff things that would melt in your mouth. She scooped those out in individual bowls and topped each with almond custard. I bet it was just loaded with calories."

Alexa got up and cleared the table. "At home we had a cook. But my mother is obsessed with maintaining her figure. My dad insisted on steak and potatoes once a week, but other than that our meals were vegetarian. I'm sorry, Rafe, I should have asked what foods you liked, instead of making you eat what I do."

"Hey, not to worry. I'm just teasing. And you did offer me steak the first night and I turned you down. If it'll make you happier, you can add chunks of beef to my vegetable kebab, and serve me meat from now until I leave."

"I can do that."

"You don't sound too thrilled. What's wrong?"

"Nothing. Nothing's wrong," she repeated.

But, there was. In just a short while, Alexa thought, Rafe would be leaving.

DOG WHINED AND PAWED at Rafe's knee. That generally meant the animal was ready to go to bed. Rafe got up and carried his plate to the sink. He had felt a definite shift in Alexa's mood. "Is everything okay?" he asked. "Your cooking's actually pretty good, you know."

"Nothing's wrong. I was just thinking I'll miss your help with the horses when you leave." She put away the pie, shooed Rafe out of the kitchen and snapped off the light. "Good night. It's going to be cold again in the morning, so we probably can do your acupuncture right after breakfast and do the outside chores later."

"Sure. That'd be good." Rafe headed down the hall but he had only taken a few steps when he stopped and called in her direction. Something was bothering him. "I'm not overly anxious to get back to Sierra's, you know."

He waited for Alexa's response, but there was nothing.

He'd really messed things up by coming on to her. Maybe she was anxious for him to go. Truth was, he'd grown comfortable here.

Comfortable with her. But Rafe wouldn't ask her if he could stay. That would be pathetic. He might be a lot of things, but he wasn't pathetic.

CHAPTER SIX

ALEXA GOT UP EARLY, showered and clipped up her hair before hurrying out to take care of morning chores. "Sheesh mineeze, it's freezing today, girls," she grumbled to the laying hens, who refused to move from their warm roosts. A thick coating of frost in spidery white lacy whorls blanketed her ranch as far as she could see. The only positive to the morning was that yesterday's biting wind had dissipated. That could signal the end of the early temperature dip.

Thankfully, she'd slept well last night under her down comforter. She hadn't been up and sitting at her computer, reviewing Rafe's case the way she did most nights. She knew he was counting on favorable results today, but Alexa wasn't a miracle worker.

She fed the horses, goats and the wildlife. The great-horned owl closed his talons around the chunk of raw beef she gave him.

His mended wing was probably strong enough to hunt, but she had to wait for a break in the weather to turn him out. He was a magnificent bird. She wanted to give him the best odds for survival.

Latching the small barn, she bent to retrieve the egg basket. A flash of color at the house drew her eye. Rafe and Compadre stood on the wide porch. Rafe held a steaming mug, which meant he'd found the teakettle and jar of instant coffee. A huge milestone in his progress in mere weeks.

As she drew closer to the porch, her heart kicked up a rapid drum beat. He looked so appealingly rumpled, not long out of bed, she was sure.

Compadre saw her and started running around in circles, barking excitedly. "Settle down." Alexa bent and scratched his wiggling backside.

"I overslept," Rafe said sheepishly. "I discovered you were gone, and Dog needed to go out. This air's frigid enough to freeze the balls off a brass monkey."

Alexa laughed as she opened the door and Compadre streaked inside.

"I tell you, I had to shove him out," Rafe

said. "That's when I decided to put on a kettle of water. Figured you'd need hot tea to warm up."

"I appreciate your thoughtfulness." She couldn't help thinking of other ways Rafe could warm her. Shaking off the enticing picture, she set the basket of eggs on the counter, then stripped off her gloves, and took off her jacket.

"After my treatment we should exercise your horses, don't you think?"

"Cold as it is, Rafe, it won't hurt to give them a day off."

He looked a little surprised. "I wouldn't have pegged you for a fair-weather rancher. What do you do when the snow starts to fly?"

"Hibernate." Alexa sighed with satisfaction when Rafe passed her a mug of piping hot peppermint tea.

"Brr. Your hands are freezing." He set his coffee on the counter and cupped his hands around hers and the mug.

It had been so long since anyone had looked after her like that. Alexa knew she should move, but didn't. They stood toe to toe until Compadre forced his shaggy head between them.

"Did you feed him?" Alexa asked, moving away from Rafe.

"No. Remember, I said he needed to go out just as I made coffee. I felt ice on the porch rail and forgot everything else. I thought maybe it'd snowed."

"Too early for snow here. But, hey, you're the one who grew up in this neck of the woods."

"I've been gone too long, I guess. I spent last winter in the Afghan mountains—it freezes a man's tonsils just to breathe there."

"It looks like a rugged, desolate country from what I've seen on podcasts. But the people are certainly beautiful. What are they like?"

"There are bad apples. Most are farmers like my folks were, only poorer. We did our best to make friends, but it's hard because we never knew who to trust."

Rafe's jaw tensed and his expression turned flat.

"Were you attacked by someone you trusted?" Alexa asked, concerned to see his hand start to shake. She curled her fingers lightly around his wrist to steady the mug he held.

"We think our guide ratted us out, but we'll never know. He died in the ambush. I try so hard to replay what happened, but, dammit, there are too many blank spots."

Alexa released his hand. "It'll come back, Rafe," she said. "You just have to be patient."

"I want to get on with the acupuncture."

"Whatever. I need breakfast first." She filled two bowls with cereal and milk and offered him one.

Rafe yanked out his chair and sat, taking the bowl from her. He tried a spoonful. "Are these grapes in my cereal?"

"Blueberries. They're loaded with free radicals."

"Which do what?" he demanded.

"I can only hope they'll improve your disposition," Alexa said, concerned that Rafe seemed to be growing more irritable.

He looked up as if he were ready to deliver a scathing comeback, but then his whole body seemed to sag. "I'm impatient."

"You think?"

"Okay, I'll eat." Rafe picked up his spoon

and dug into his granola. "Has anyone ever told you you'd make a good drill sergeant?"

Alexa clenched her spoon. Was that how Rafe saw her? As a taskmaster? "I'm sorry, Rafe. But if you're too tense, we can't do your treatment."

Compadre trotted up to Rafe and batted at his thigh a few times before nosing under the fingers Rafe thrummed on his knee. "All right. I know when I'm outnumbered."

They finished breakfast in silence then Alexa took their bowls to the sink. She glanced out the window to see a pale sun already melting the frost off the roof. "You know, Rafe, it seems to be warming up a bit. We were cooped up inside yesterday and I think we both need to unwind. What do you say to a short trail ride?"

"I say you're stalling on my treatment," Rafe said bluntly. "But it does sound good. Let me grab my sweatshirt."

Alexa had to admit that she might be stalling. But Rafe seemed wound pretty tight this morning, and riding did relax him. She readied a saddlebag for the trip, and by the time she'd finished and stepped onto the porch, Rafe joined her.

Compadre followed him out. "You have to stay, Dog," Rafe said.

"If we don't ride in the park, he can come, Rafe. There are trails in the Christmas Mountains. This time of year we should have them to ourselves. I threw apples and water in a saddlebag, and I can add kibble for Compadre. If I ride Gigi, she's fine with me hooking a rope to the dog's collar. That'll ensure he doesn't run off chasing rabbits."

Rafe knelt and scrubbed the dog's head. "That sounds good. He wants to go, don't you, guy?"

Alexa went back inside for the kibble. Minutes later they entered the barn, where Rafe saddled Loki with practiced ease.

"Good job," Alexa said as she climbed on Gigi. "I told you saddling a horse is like riding a bicycle, Rafe. It's a skill you never forget."

"It felt good to land a saddle on Loki's back the first time," he admitted. "I've missed riding. It was such a big part of my life before I went into the army. You know, Alexa, much as I want my next treatment, I admit I'm strung tight as a fiddle."

Alexa grinned to herself. With a snap of the reins, she urged Gigi into a trot.

Rafe caught up. "Aren't you going to say *I told you so*?"

"I'm too pleased by how far you've come from the silent, stone-faced man Sierra delivered to my ranch."

Rafe hung back as she sped up, and Alexa worried that maybe she'd spoken too soon. She kept glancing back, and so did Compadre.

Eventually Rafe drew his horse abreast of hers. "What happened to the sun?"

"It's hidden behind a tree-topped ridge. If you're cold we can turn back, Rafe."

He wrapped his reins around the saddle horn and zipped up his heavy sweatshirt. He was in the process of groping again for the reins when Loki tossed his head a couple of times, whinnied, and began a sideways hop back down the trail. The gelding backed into Alexa's horse.

At first, she didn't know what was happening. It took a moment to control Gigi. By then Loki was blowing, snorting and rearing, and Compadre lunged against his rope, barking crazily.

"What's going on?" Rafe asked anxiously. "Alexa? I can't find but one damned rein. Did it drop and tangle in Dog's rope? What's happening?"

"Coyotes," Alexa said in a low voice, doing her best to keep her skittish mare on the trail. "I count five, Rafe. That's a big pack." She couldn't keep the panic from her voice. "A hunting pack, I'd say from the way they've split on either side of the trail. I've never known coyotes to attack humans, but this cold snap's probably driven a lot of their food underground. Compadre," she ordered sternly, "settle down."

"Did you hear me say I dropped a rein?" Rafe attempted to control Loki by grabbing hold of his mane. But the gelding would have none of that. A big horse, he dug his back hooves into the soft red clay and all but sat on his haunches as he pawed the air. His right hoof clipped Alexa's shoulder as she forced Gigi closer in an attempt to scoop up Rafe's loose rein. The lead coyotes ran ahead on the trail and began circling, which sent Compadre into an even greater frenzy.

On the third try, Alexa managed to snag Loki's rein. "Sit still, Rafe, and hang on," she said, panting from the exertion of trying to steady the dog and the extra horse. "I'll turn both horses, and we'll blast past the coyotes. I doubt they'll follow us to the clearing." Loki and Gigi bumped rumps and kicked out at one another.

"Dammit, I feel useless." Rafe swore roundly a second time when stirrups tangled with Alexa's. His swearing sent the coyote pair nearest the horses slinking off into the trees.

"Good going, Rafe—you scared off two coyotes," Alexa told him through gritted teeth. "Okay, I've got us turned around. But we have three stubborn coyotes keeping pace to our left. Now's the time to let out a rebel yell if you know any, Rafe."

"That I do," Rafe said. His raucous yodel echoed off the ridge and set the coyotes yipping off after their pack mates, but Compadre gave chase, doubling back under Gigi's belly. His wild barking frightened an already agitated Loki, who proceeded to buck Rafe off. He slid ten feet or so in the soft, wet red clay and came to a stop face-first on a bed of pine needles.

"Oh my God, Rafe." Alexa vaulted out of her saddle. "Are you all right?" In her haste, she lost her tenuous hold on Loki's rein, and he galloped off down the trail.

Sitting up, Rafe spat out dirt and pine needles around a steady stream of curses that had Alexa cringing.

"Tell me you didn't break any bones," she said, shakily brushing twigs and leaves out of Rafe's hair and off his shoulders.

He shook off her hands and stood up. "What's hurt is my pride," he snarled. "Where are those damned coyotes?"

Alexa shifted Gigi's reins and Compadre's rope to her left hand. "I think they took off. Our Abbott and Costello routine was too much for them. But Loki ran off, too. If only your pride hurts, Rafe, we need to double up and go find him."

"Will the mare handle our combined weight?"

She pictured them riding spooned together and it wasn't the extra burden on the horse that concerned her. "You'll have to squeeze on behind me, Rafe." It would be more comfortable if he sat in front, but Alexa needed to see. He'd probably realize that and feel really useless. The trail ride she had hoped would relax him was going to have the opposite effect.

RAFE MOUNTED WITHOUT help. He even pulled Alexa up. They were wedged tight together in the saddle. He wrapped his fingers in the fabric of her jacket, and by the time Gigi took two steps down the trail, the friction of Alexa's butt in the cradle of his thighs took Rafe's mind off the humiliating incident and sent it in a new direction. If she noticed the discomfort their riding double caused him, she didn't show it. She rattled on, fretting about losing Loki. He gritted his teeth and tried to scoot back against the cantle.

"Rafe?" Alexa turned slightly. "Are you brooding over being dumped off Loki? It wasn't your fault."

The agony Rafe was experiencing had nothing to do with the fall, but Alexa's comment served to refocus his attention. "I'm a three-time national bronc riding champion. It's a little ego bruising to be dumped by a good-natured riding horse."

Every so often Rafe's unshaven jaw caught in Alexa's hair and it was all he could do to keep from burying his face in the warm, sweet-smelling strands. She was so much smaller than he was, and he wanted to draw

her back against him and take the reins. Damn
his blindness.

"I knew the fall was eating at you," she
said. "Accidents happen, Rafe."

Each time her soft curls blew back and tickled his face, he felt a sweet heat burn straight
down between his thighs. If he dipped his
head just slightly forward, he could press his
lips into the delicate curve of her neck. Rafe
forced another inch between them. Being near
Alexa made him horny as hell, and he didn't
give a rat's ass about doctor-patient trust.
Nothing could keep him from wanting to get
her naked. He had it bad.

"There he is," Alexa exclaimed suddenly,
cutting into Rafe's thoughts. "Loki's waiting
at the corral, docile as a kitten, the goofball.
Why don't I let you off here at the house,
Rafe? You can take Compadre inside. I'm sure
you want a shower. I'll put up the horses, then
come in and fix lunch. I swear, Rafe, I feel so
bad. I envisioned us riding up to the butte for
lunch."

He dismounted behind her, his body
screaming from pain, and not just from his
tumble off Loki. That ride had been pure

torture. He only hoped he could get his body back under control before their scheduled treatment.

ALEXA'S CELL PHONE RANG as she was putting away the remains of their lunch. "Mother," she exclaimed after stretching to scoop up the phone from the counter. "Is everything all right with Daddy?" Her mother never called during the day. She was too busy with her charities.

"At a fundraiser your father and I attended Saturday, Dr. Levinson asked about you," Kate Robinson said in her low, well modulated voice. "Driving home, Jason noted we hadn't heard from you in a month. Are you okay, Alexa?"

Obviously her mother hadn't been worried. She'd waited until Tuesday to check up on her daughter. "I'm fine, Mother. Just busy."

"Doing what?" Kate pressed.

Rafe walked back into the kitchen just then.

"What did you say, Alexa?"

She covered the speaker and hissed that she was on the phone. Then she turned away from him. "I'm training new horses, Mother," she said. "And a park ranger brought me two baby foxes that take a lot of care. I probably should go now. Tell Daddy I said hi."

But her mother droned on about a new hospital committee she chaired. "Your father wants to visit you. But honestly, Alexa, between the wind farm he's setting up and my meetings, we can't find two consecutive days free. You live so far out in the boonies. And before you scold me, I said the same thing when your grandparents were alive. You simply must come to Houston for Thanksgiving. The Wednesday prior we're hosting an open house, but it's a small gathering. Thirty or so of Jason's employees."

"Don't count on me, Mother," Alexa stressed. "I can't leave the animals."

"Surely you can get one of your neighbors to check on them."

Alexa sighed. "They've all got enough of their own work and there's no one exactly nearby."

"You always have an excuse," her mother protested. "And I know the real reason. But, dear, people have forgotten the incident with the Duval boy. It's been five years. It's time you get back to civilization. There are a few nice, eligible young men working with your father."

Alexa felt a queasy dip in her stomach. "I'll think about Thanksgiving. Bye, Mother." She hung up before Kate could reply. Alexa's mother collected tons of money for her favorite charities because she never took no for an answer.

Rafe was leaning against the refrigerator, just staring her way. He couldn't see her, but Alexa couldn't help wondering what her mother would say if Alexa had told her she had an eligible young man staying at the ranch who kept her awake most nights?

"Does your mother know you have a houseguest who could feed your animals over Thanksgiving?" Rafe asked.

Alexa swallowed guiltily. "I...ah...didn't tell her because you'll be leaving soon."

"Oh. Are you sure I won't need more than one month of acupuncture treatments?"

"There isn't a set recommended number, Rafe."

"I get it. You want me to leave when the month is up, whether or not we're making progress."

"No, it's not that." She rubbed suddenly

sweating palms up and down the side of her jeans. Before Bobby, she would have known instinctively whether Rafe's treatments should be stopped or continued. But now she needed results to rely on.

"What time is it?" Rafe asked unexpectedly.

Alexa consulted her watch. "A quarter after two."

Rafe shoved away from the fridge. "Before you're interrupted again, shall we get started with the acupuncture?"

"Are you sure you don't want to wait a day after your fall?"

"I'm fine. I need you to tell me if my chest is bruised." He slid a hand up and down his breastbone.

Merely thinking about his bare chest made Alexa's face flush. It was a good thing Rafe couldn't see her. "I…ah…you took a bone-jarring jolt."

"Can't you mix up some of your herbs to make a cream?"

"Devil's claw," she said, opening the door to her office. "It's a potent anti-inflammatory. I can mix some up if you need it."

"Or you could massage my chest with that

warm oil you use on my back," he said suggestively.

"Okay, enough with that, Rafe." Was he deliberately baiting her? If so, it was working. She slapped a hand on the examining table. "If I think you're bruised, I'll prepare a muscle cream you can put on before you go to bed."

He stripped off his shirt and lay down. "I wish I could see if I make you blush. I think I do. Are you hiding behind your ethics, doctor?"

Alexa stopped in the middle of pulling on sterile gloves. His carelessly tossed barb had found its mark, though not the one he'd intended. But he didn't know about Bobby, so he had no idea how much his remark hurt her. "Behave yourself," she said, trying to keep her voice light.

"Yes, ma'am." He gave a dutiful response. "But what if I said you can massage cream or oil into any part of my body you'd like, Alexa?"

His thick-as-honey drawl sent warning tingles straight to Alexa's stomach, and given the sweet torture she'd endured on their ride home with Rafe's aroused body behind hers it was time they ended this banter. "Rafe, don't mess with a woman holding a handful of sharp objects."

His laugh was purely masculine.

She had to work extra hard to keep her hands steady. Because of that, she took greater care placing each needle.

Rafe didn't fall asleep during this session. He was too keyed up.

"Lie still," Alexa cautioned for the third time. "Empty your mind of negative thoughts."

"Oh, my thoughts aren't negative," he said.

"I'm going to stop and light a couple of candles. They're chamomile, lemon balm and linden flower. I want you to breathe deeply and picture yourself floating in water."

"Are you floating with me? Are we naked?"

"Rafe!"

What was the matter with him? It was as if he'd crossed an imaginary line she'd drawn in the sand.

Alexa tossed down her gloves. Her hand shook as she lit the candles, directing the thin trail of smoke toward the table.

"Ouch, I felt that." His smile disappeared and he reached for a spot behind his ear. He was stopped by Alexa's sharp command. "Don't touch. I'm sorry if it hurt. I think you're still unstrung from the fall. We should stop here."

"No, please. I'll lie still."

Alexa watched his body go limp. That let her work, but left her mind free to appreciate his smooth bronzed chest. She knew for a fact she had never had a sexual attraction to any of her former patients. It was cool in the room, but she started to perspire. Several times, she had to pause and use her sleeve to blot her forehead. Rafe Eaglefeather was too potent for his own good. Or for hers.

When at last she finished, she stepped away from the table. "The session is over, Rafe. I need to apply tape to a few spots. I'll remove it tonight."

He opened his eyes, sat up and scanned the room. "There's no change from what I could see after the last treatment." His voice was heavy with disappointment.

Alexa extinguished the candles. Her own heart felt heavy, and she couldn't express her sorrow.

"I'd hoped..." Rafe said, then he slid off the table and reached for his shirt.

"I know, Rafe. Me, too. We'll try again Friday. Or maybe I should call Dr. Ling. He's the Chinese master in Houston I studied under. Maybe he'd be willing to take over your treatments."

What if she'd lost her skill with the needles? The Houston media had accused her of being a sham. What if they were right?

"If Ling taught you everything he knows, how could he do any more than you can, Alexa?" Rafe's voice was muffled as he struggled to pull an army shirt over his head without unbuttoning it.

"Here, let me help. I don't want you dislodging the tape strips."

Rafe flapped his arms. "I'm stuck."

"Stop." She unbuttoned the shirt far enough for him to poke his head through, then rebuttoned it, letting her hands trail down Rafe's chest.

He caught her hands in his. "I prefer the shirts you bought that have snaps. I must have grabbed a uniform shirt by mistake. I probably shouldn't wear it since I'm a civilian now."

"Someone removed all the identifying

badges. You'd have to look really close to see their outline. Otherwise it looks like any old khaki shirt."

Still holding Alexa's hands flat against his chest, Rafe said, "Sierra must have ripped off the patches. She's a saver. She learned it from our mom."

"Given the shape of the economy it's a good way to live."

"Are you doing okay, Alexa? Financially, I mean. I expect to pay for room and board, and for your services."

Alexa jerked back her hands and put some distance between them. "I told Sierra money wasn't the issue if I let you come here, Rafe. You're working Esperanza, after all. I do fine financially training and selling horses. Technically I don't have a formal holistic practice here."

"Why not?"

This was getting into territory Alexa just didn't want to discuss, especially with Rafe. "You said yourself, I live off the beaten path. And I like what I do."

"You have a nice ranch from what I can tell. I'd say you're doing okay, Alexa."

"I'm doing fine, Rafe." Eager to change the

subject, Alexa said, "I thought we could eat by the fire again. I have more country-western CDs."

"Sounds good. But can you remove this tape from my forehead?"

"Bugging you, huh? If you promise not to rub the spots, I'll take the tape off."

Alexa made a vegetable stir-fry dish with rice, and after they were finished, Compadre fell asleep in front of the fireplace, and Alexa picked up the Twain book again. Rafe couldn't seem to sit still. "What time is it now?" he asked for about the third time in half an hour.

"Six-forty," she said. "I'm on the last story in my book."

"Since it's still too early to hit the hay, why don't you read to me? What's the name of the story anyway?"

"The Man Who Corrupted Hadleyburg."

"Sound's good."

Alexa turned the page and began to read.

Rafe moved to the end of the couch closer to her chair, and crossed his long legs at the ankle. The way he kept time to the music with his foot distracted Alexa. He distracted her.

She finished the story at the same time the CD ended, and got up to change the music.

Rafe's eyes were half closed, but Alexa knew he wasn't asleep. "This is a collection of golden-oldie blues tunes by well-known country artists," she said. "What do you suppose there is about living in the south that makes cowboys sing the blues?"

"The best places to sing the blues are during a war or in jail, staring into the bottom of an empty whiskey glass or facing an empty bed," Rafe said.

Alexa hit the play button. "Tell me you're not an authority on all those situations."

"All but jail. Hey, turn up the sound. Come dance with me. I know this room fairly well, and hardwood's good for waltzing." He stood up and beckoned Alexa with outstretched arms. "Next to riding horses, cowboys love to dance."

Alexa held back. "Uh, I can't. I mean I've never been very good at dancing. And I haven't danced in years."

"Ah, finally something I can teach you," he said, approaching her and pulling her into his arms. "You know how I'm supposed to loosen up before acupuncture? Same goes for dancing. Lean against me and put your head on my shoulder, Alexa. Feel the music. Move when I move."

"Sorry, but I'm not short enough to put my head on your shoulder."

"Then tuck your ear up next to mine. Did I ever tell you I like tall women?"

"Uh, I don't believe so." Alexa cordoned off the part of her mind that was telling her this was a big mistake. To Rafe she said, "Don't blame me if I step all over your boots."

"Shh. Listen to the music. I like holding you. Pretend you like holding me."

Alexa didn't respond, but snuggled in. It was actually on the tip of her tongue to say she didn't need to pretend. The words melted there when Rafe slid both of his hands around her waist. It wasn't long before he nuzzled her cheek with his lips.

Sighing, she slid both palms flat against his chest.

For several long riffs of a moody guitar, she gazed sleepily into Rafe's gorgeous eyes. She willed him to see her. Willed him to see the world. Without sight he was missing so many beautiful things in life. And if her treatments helped him see again, that would restore her faith in herself. Unable to stop herself, she moved even closer to Rafe.

His lips grazed her ear, and in a husky voice Rafe sang along with the CD, the words haunting and provocative. Alexa trembled in his arms.

"Tonight let's just be a man and a woman, Alexa. Not doctor and patient. We'll be two lovers with nothing in mind and just shut out the world…lose ourselves in hot, sweaty sex."

Alexa's mind had long since shut down. The music grew fainter as blood pumped louder in her ears. And in her heart. Then all at once it dawned on her that Rafe had slow danced her down the hall and into his room. Light from the hall outlined his rumpled bed as if it sat in the glare of a spotlight. Warning bells went off inside her fuzzy brain.

"Wait. Rafe, what are you doing? I told you any type of a romantic relationship between us is out of the question."

"You seemed ready enough a minute ago." Releasing her, Rafe threw up his hands. "I didn't hide my intentions, Alexa. You sure as hell send off mixed messages." He wheeled away, and his hands curled and uncurled at his sides.

Frustrated, and steeped in guilt herself for wanting Rafe, Alexa recognized that the line she'd drawn between being a doctor and a woman wasn't as clear as it should be. "Rafe," she finally blurted. "We just can't seem to keep things professional. It's not your fault, but you need to find another practitioner. I know you want more acupuncture treatments, but you'll have to look elsewhere. It's best if you leave with Sierra when she comes next week."

When Rafe said nothing, Alexa left his room and raced toward her own. She skirted Compadre, who padded down the hall toward Rafe.

Alexa wasn't the only one who would miss Rafe when he was gone.

CHAPTER SEVEN

RAFE WANTED TO STAY HERE. He'd known it for some time now but hadn't wanted to admit it. And after tonight, it was clear that his feelings for Alexa weren't one-sided. But he had crossed the line she had drawn. Tonight, he'd been restless and discouraged about his treatment. Alexa had been caught up in the bluesy music so they'd both been vulnerable.

He propped his back against the pillows and crossed his arms behind his head, unable to sleep. If he was honest, it was Alexa, not his mood or the music that had aroused him. She had all the qualities he admired in a woman. Intelligence. Feistiness. Humor. Independence. And with Alexa there was an added plus. She loved horses. He could count on one hand the number of women in his past who came close to Alexa. His previous relationships had all eventually fizzled, ended by distance or a clash in careers. In one case, the woman wanted a man who wasn't running around foreign lands getting shot at. Military rules regarding fraternization also made it easy for him to walk away when he wasn't interested. But, the real truth was, with all those women, he hadn't been committed enough to make concessions. Now he was. Dammit, his feelings for Alexa weren't superficial. They ran a helluva lot deeper than a mere one-night stand. That he was sure of.

But Alexa didn't want to treat him anymore. Was that really about ethics? Earlier today she hadn't mentioned his being here to her mother. He didn't think it was simple oversight.

Something else was troubling Alexa— holding her back—other than ethics. He hadn't imagined the heat rising off both of them tonight. It was hot enough to scorch the ceiling.

Just thinking about it guaranteed him a restless night.

SOMEONE WAS NUZZLING his ear. Rafe jerked awake, his heart tripping happily, to Dog nudging him. As he swung out of bed, Rafe recalled every sizzling detail of a dream he'd had involving bedroom games he wanted to play with Alexa. And it wasn't just the prospect of sex that drove him, though that sure played a part. He longed to continue the everyday things they did together, like training her horses, sitting by the fire. In the cold light of day, Rafe knew he wanted to settle down with Alexa Robinson. But what did a man like him really have to offer a woman like her? Maybe in the end she was right. She was his doctor and he was her patient.

He headed for the shower and let a stream of cold water shock him back to reality. When that didn't change his feelings about Alexa, he decided he had to leave with Sierra. If he cut the doctor-patient ties with Alexa, maybe he could figure a way to make her see him as a man.

He went to breakfast, prepared to tell her his next acupuncture session on Friday would be the final one. In the kitchen he discovered she'd set out granola and milk, and his dishes. He assumed hers were already in the dishwasher.

Rather than eat, he pulled on a sweatshirt and went out to the barn to find Alexa, but Dog kept nudging him back toward the house. Eventually, he found her holed up in her office.

"I'm working," she called when he rattled the doorknob of a locked door. "I left breakfast on the table for you."

"I know. I just came to say I'll be leaving with Sierra on Saturday. Or I can call her to come earlier if you'd prefer. Myself, I'd rather have you do one last round of acupuncture on Friday. All strictly professional, of course."

Rafe heard her unlock the door and open it a crack. "As long as we're on the same page and there are no repeats of last night, I don't have a problem with you staying until Sierra's scheduled pickup."

The door creaked open a little farther, and though he couldn't see her features, Rafe sensed a nervous edginess in Alexa and would bet a month's salary that she hadn't got any more sleep than him.

"Shall I put Esperanza through her barrels?" he asked Alexa. This wasn't the time to share his real reason for leaving—so he could try to move forward in a real romantic relationship.

"Work with the mare or not, Rafe. She's

probably trained well enough now to go to the man who'd like to buy her for his daughter."

"Oh. Well, it's warmed up outside. Esperanza and Tano will be full of energy."

"Is it warmer? I haven't been out yet. I'll exercise Tano later." She sounded preoccupied, which struck Rafe as odd. Usually by this hour she would have fed the wild animals and the horses.

"Are you okay?" He shouldn't pry. Questions of a personal nature could lead him down a slippery slope. But Rafe wanted them to part on good terms, and if she felt she needed to keep a door between them, he had to rectify that.

"I'm working, Rafe. I have paperwork to catch up on. Just because I treat you in my home doesn't mean I'm lax about keeping records. You'll leave here with a comprehensive file. Whoever you continue treatment with may not approve of alternative medicine, but every therapy, every treatment I did will be spelled out in black and white."

Whoa! Where did all this defensiveness come from?

"Jeez, Alexa. When I landed on your doorstep, I didn't give a rip about any kind of treatment. Physically I've improved a lot. And if my eyesight's as good as it'll get, I may not even have to see another doctor."

He could sense her hesitation. "Whatever you do is your business, Rafe. But new discoveries happen every day in medicine. Please, try not to settle for anything less than a full recovery."

Rafe nodded his agreement and turned to head out to the barn.

He didn't plan to settle for anything less. And that meant having Alexa. But for the moment, he would keep his little secret to himself.

RAFE COOLED ESPERANZA down after she traversed the barrels numerous times without bumping any of them. He'd stalled ending her session as he waited for Alexa to bring Tano out. Twenty minutes or so ago she'd gone into the wild-animal barn. He knew the fox kits were eating on their own, so Rafe wasn't sure what was keeping her. He'd heard her go in and out. Maybe she was cleaning cages. He'd been here long enough to know Alexa did that when she wanted to avoid him.

At last she brought Tano into the corral.

"I thought you'd be done," she said abruptly. "I left you a sprout and tomato sandwich in the fridge for lunch. I'll eat after I'm through working Tano."

"Is it lunchtime?" Rafe led the mare over to join Alexa at the barn entrance. Rafe had one hand on Esperanza's muzzle and could feel the horses rub noses in greeting.

"It's one o'clock," Alexa said. "Actually, it's almost fifteen past."

Their exchange was interrupted by the sound of auto tires crunching down Alexa's private lane.

"You have a visitor," Rafe noted, lifting his head and straining to listen. "More than one vehicle would be my guess. Are you expecting company?"

"No. But you're right. There are two vehicles. The lead one looks like Sierra's van. Did you ask her to pick you up today?"

"No. I told you, I want my acupuncture treatment Friday. Hmm. Sierra's not one to travel this far from home during the week when Curt and Chloe are in kindergarten. I hope nothing's wrong with anyone in the family." Rafe's shoulders tensed. Doug's job as a border patrol agent was dangerous at times.

"I hope not, too," Alexa murmured. "It is Sierra," she clarified a moment later. "She doesn't appear panicked. She's walking back to a white compact that pulled in behind her. An older woman is in that car. I think Sierra spotted you, Rafe. Why don't I take Esperanza to her stall for you?"

Rafe tightened his hold on the mare's halter. "Is the other woman short and dark-haired? It might be Doug's mother. I call her Tía Maria. The Martinezes were our closest neighbors."

"The woman's not Hispanic. She's tall and has gray hair and she's wearing a blue suit. She's getting out a…briefcase from the car."

"Doesn't sound like anyone I know," Rafe said, frowning.

"They've opened the corral gate and are heading this way." Alexa relieved Rafe of the mare's reins. "I'll stall both horses, and be right back. No doubt they want to see you, Rafe."

He headed toward the house. Sierra hurried over to meet him, giving him a quick hug. "Rafe, this is Ms. Holmes. She's from the VA."

There was a note of panic in Sierra's voice but Rafe couldn't ask her about it with the other woman there.

Ms. Holmes spoke with a nasal twang. "Our department doesn't make a habit of hunting down wayward patients, Major Eaglefeather. But after I spoke to your sister, my supervisor made an exception in your case."

"I'm doing fine," Rafe said. "Sierra should have given you my cell number. We could have handled any questions you have via the phone."

"You've missed two counseling appointments and a post-surgery checkup," the woman said. "But when Mrs. Martinez informed me you'd placed yourself under the care of a local healer..." Rafe couldn't miss the disapproval in her voice. "I wrote down the information. Luckily, my assistant recognized Dr. Robinson's name. It's obvious neither you, Major, nor your sister are aware she closed her practice in Houston...after she killed a patient by the name of Bobby Duval through gross negligence."

"I swear I heard only good things about the

doctor from park rangers and border patrol agents, including my husband," Sierra objected. "Rafe, you have to come home with me today. If you suffer a single ill effect from anything she…the doctor did, I'll never forgive myself."

"Stop it, Sierra. Do I look worse off?" Rafe couldn't believe what he was hearing.

"N-no. I think you've put on some much needed weight. And—"

"Well, then," Rafe interrupted gruffly.

"I suggest when you two get home, Mrs. Martinez, that you look up the newspaper accounts from the Houston paper's archives," Ms. Holmes said. "Now, we should get you rescheduled, Major Eaglefeather. I can make an appointment at the VA in San Antonio or Houston for next week."

Sierra squeezed his arm. "Rafe…?"

For an awkward moment, Rafe vacillated. He'd planned to leave when Sierra came for him on Saturday, but he had every intention of coming back. He wanted a different kind of relationship with Alexa, but he hadn't figured out the details yet. This morning as he put Esperanza through her paces, he pictured staying here with Alexa—forever. But he wasn't ready to lay that one on her yet, especially in front of others. One thing he did know beyond a shadow of doubt was that Ms. Holmes was flat-assed wrong. Alexa couldn't have killed anyone. Yet with those ugly accusations, how could he walk away from her now? "I'm not going back to the VA," he said. "That much I know. They can take a flying leap, Sierra."

"I've packed your duffel, Rafe." It was Alexa. How much had she overheard? She forced the bag into his hands. "You should take Ms. Holmes's advice and use every service the VA has to offer. Now, if you'll all excuse me," she said, her voice quivering with tension, "I have a great horned owl to release into the wild."

With a snap of her fingers, she commanded Compadre to her side. Rafe could hear her march off down the path toward the wild-animal barn. Why hadn't she defended herself? It was all he could do not to go after her. But Rafe realized he needed to be away from here to figure out what his next move should be.

No way would he blow his chances with Alexa. There were still a lot of uncertainties in his life, but he knew one thing for sure. The only future he wanted would be shared with Alexa.

ALEXA WATCHED THE VEHICLES head down the lane. Compadre barked sharply. He left her side and loped a few yards down the path, then stopped and swung his head around to look at her. Trotting back to her, the collie flopped on his belly and whined deep in his throat before burying his nose in his paws.

"Don't look at me with those cow eyes," Alexa said, mopping her own tears. She crouched down beside him. "I'm sorry, Compadre. I'm going to miss Rafe, too."

It was the truth. Alexa had known for a while that Rafe meant more to her than a patient should. But there was no way she would go after him and bring him back.

"It's best for him to leave." Alexa gave the dog a final pat and stood up, tucking her hands in her back pockets. "Maybe when he's examined by new doctors, they'll discover something that was missed. Something to get Rafe's sight back."

Watching Rafe leave had been so hard. But if she'd bared her soul to him, told her side of the story about Bobby, he would have felt obligated to stay out of pity. That was the kind of caring man she'd learned he was. And the last thing she wanted from Rafe was pity. "I want him to stay out of trust. Or…or out of… love," she murmured aloud to Compadre.

What a mess she'd gotten herself into. Yes, Rafe wanted to sleep with her. But, did he care about her? About Alexa Robinson the woman. Or was it just their shared proximity of the past few weeks and the fact she'd set him on the road to healing that had made the sexual attraction flare?

She couldn't face releasing the great-horned owl today. What if freedom led to his death in the wild? She'd come to love that bird and needed to be strong when she set him free. And she wasn't strong today. She'd already lost too much.

RAFE SAID NEXT TO NOTHING on the drive to his sister's place. He shut his eyes and leaned against the headrest. The twins kept asking their mother what was wrong with their Uncle Rafe, but Sierra shushed them.

At last they stopped at the school to pick up Curt and Chloe from kindergarten.

When they reached the house, Sierra told Rafe that little had changed. "Doug's working a lot of overtime," Sierra said, "so he hasn't done much on the addition."

All four kids raced outside to play. "Rafe, I put your duffel in the hall closet where it was before. I'll make the sofa bed up after supper." He could sense her hesitation. "Rafe, I take full responsibility for sending you to Dr. Robinson. I am so, so sorry."

Rafe slashed out a hand, putting an end to Sierra's words. "I don't know what happened in Houston with Alexa's practice, but I'm damned sure it wasn't her fault."

"Then…I don't get it, Rafe." Sierra sounded confused. "Don't you want to be here? But… we're your family, Rafe."

He buried his balled fists in his front pockets. "The day after I got there, Alexa made me pick up a chair I knocked over. She taught me to count steps so I could get around inside and out without bumping into stuff. I rode a horse by myself, and I helped train one. I told you—after one acupuncture treatment I can see shadows. I just don't believe she killed anyone by being negligent. She's a pro, and I've never met a more compassionate woman."

"Ah." Sierra hooked her arm through Rafe's and steered him to the kitchen. "I think I'm beginning to clue in here. So just when did you fall in love with Dr. Robinson, Rafe?"

His sister's blunt statement poleaxed Rafe. He stuttered and stammered, but couldn't come up with a word to say.

Sierra dragged him into the kitchen. "Sit here, and I'll put on a pot of coffee. Then we'll have a real heart-to-heart."

Rafe had learned as a kid it was futile to argue with his sister. Sierra had the tenacity of a mongoose.

When the coffee finished dripping and she'd poured each of them a cup, she took her usual seat opposite Rafe. Reaching across the table, she directed his hand to his mug. "Okay, give it up. I'd ask if Alexa took advantage of you, but everything you said a minute ago tells me that's wrong thinking."

"It was the opposite." Rafe blew on his coffee. "I was the one who tried to make a move on Alexa, but she threw up the doctor-patient roadblock. I'm pretty sure she didn't want to object—that it was only on principle.

I think we'd be good together, Sierra. Alexa gave me confidence to want to live again."

"Are you sure she was interested that way, Rafe? Maybe she just considers herself your doctor? I figured she'd be the one to hit on you. I mean, losing your sight hasn't made you less a man than you were when you won bronc riding championships. You're a handsome guy, Rafe, and you've got a great heart. I won't stand for her or anyone else rejecting you or hurting you."

Rafe grinned. "You're too protective of me, Sierra." Rafe took a swig of his beverage.

"You're the only little brother I have. I'll always fight for what's best for you."

"I'm not so little anymore," Rafe said gently. "You don't have to fight my battles."

"But…but she might break your heart."

"Or I might break hers. You know, I don't even know what Alexa looks like. Not that it matters to me."

"She's pretty. Blonde. Her hair is shoulder length. I remember thinking she has the bluest eyes of anyone I've ever met. She's taller than me. Almost as tall as you. A lot skinnier than me, too," Sierra concluded ruefully.

Recalling earlier conversations he'd had

with Alexa, Rafe suddenly asked, "If you compared her to a movie star, who would it be?"

"Oh, gosh." Sierra paused a minute. "I'd say Cameron Diaz off the top of my head." Reaching out, she poked Rafe in acknowledgment of the slow smile spreading across his face. "Okay, so now you know your doctor is a babe, how do you propose to get back into her life? She didn't exactly stop you from leaving—almost shoved you out the door."

"That's the problem, Sierra…I can't go back there as Alexa's patient. But it just occurred to me…maybe I could convince her to take me back as a ranch hand. Do you think Doug can drive me back there tomorrow?"

"He's down south on patrol for a few days. How about next week? That's if you still feel the same then. Rafe…I think we should find out more about that Bobby Duval guy. I bet I can use the church computer."

"No," Rafe said emphatically. "If Alexa wants to tell me, fine. Otherwise we'll leave it be. Lord knows I'm not guilt-free."

"You didn't kill anyone."

He wrapped both hands tightly around his cup.

His sister's voice was low but determined. "War is different, Rafe."

"I said leave it, Sierra." She didn't have a chance to reply because at that moment he snapped the handle off his cup.

ALEXA MOPED ABOUT her ranch all weekend. The weather had turned foul on Saturday. Dark gray clouds hung low, threatening to rain. So once again she delayed releasing the owl. His wing seemed healed, but after Ms. Holmes's reminder, Alexa wasn't sure she had the expertise to heal anyone, human or animal.

Sunday night she had trouble sleeping. The November wind picked up and something banged against the house. Restless, she knew the power could go out, but still she got out of bed and booted up her computer. It was a good night to research whether any new information on blindness had come out in the monthly medical journals.

Turning up nothing of interest, Alexa clicked through a few military medical sites and found an article posted by the navy about a study that Rafe might qualify for. The lights flickered and she hurriedly shut down her computer. The truth was, Rafe was no longer her patient. He was back under the VA's care. If his doctors thought it beneficial, they'd see he got considered for the study. It was time for her to step back.

EARLY MONDAY, ALEXA went out to pick up limbs brought down by the night's storm. At this time of year storms blew in and out capriciously. She found the source of the banging and righted the empty feed barrel.

Compadre dug into a fresh gopher hole, but all he got for his effort was a dirty snout. Alexa brushed his nose clean, and he followed her into the horse barn. She was in the middle of measuring out grain when she heard a vehicle pull in. A ripple of excitement ran through her. Could it be Rafe coming back?

She ran out of the barn, Compadre at her heels. It was a letdown to see a white pickup with a forestry insignia on the driver's door.

Alexa steeled herself for another run-in with Paul Goodman. But the man who climbed out of the pickup was Carl Dobbins, the ranger who had brought her the mountain cats.

He hailed her and they met on the path. "Howdy, Alexa. I finally found a home for the cats with a reputable zoo. Had to cut through red tape. How are the little buggers?"

"They've grown. I wondered if you planned to return them to the wild. I've tried not to get cozy with them, but it was hard. They were so cuddly."

"I didn't think they'd survive a winter in the high country being hand-fed."

"I agree. You can go on into the wild-animal barn. I'll shut my dog up until you load the cats."

He nodded and continued on to the smaller barn.

"Sorry, Compadre. Carl doesn't need you barking and stirring up the cats."

The dog always acted as if he was being punished whenever she closed him in the barn and left him. Alexa suspected he'd been mistreated in the past. Because of that she took the time to scratch his ears and pet him. "I'll only be gone a minute," she promised.

"You're not kidding these guys have grown," Dobbins said as Alexa joined him at the cages. He hefted one, and Alexa picked up the other. "Can you manage that alone?" he asked.

"I load and unload hay bales that weigh more than this, Carl."

They headed outside together. As he put his cage in the back of his pickup, Carl said, "I heard a rumor you'd hired an ex-soldier to help out. Somebody said he was disabled. Blind. But you know how rumors get out of hand."

Alexa stiffened. "I didn't hire him. His sister hoped alternative medical treatments might restore his sight. He helped me train horses while he was here, and really had a knack. Probably because he used to be on the rodeo circuit before he was a soldier. A grand national bronc riding champion, in fact."

"You don't mean Rafe Eaglefeather?"

"Yes. Do you know him?"

"Know of him. Saw him ride a number of times. I recall reading in the Lajitas newspaper that he'd joined the army. A group of rodeo cowboys did. I'm sorry as hell to hear Eaglefeather came home wounded. Any chance he'll ever see again?"

"I don't know, Carl. That will be up to VA doctors."

"From all the stories I've read about our returning heroes, too many are falling through the cracks. If you see him again, tell him an old rodeo fan wishes him well."

Because Alexa found it hard to swallow, she just nodded.

Carl closed and latched his tailgate. "I'd better hit the road with these guys. It's a long drive to Houston."

Alexa watched the dual-wheeled pickup turn around. She remained standing in the same spot until it disappeared from sight.

She didn't want Rafe falling through any cracks. A fear that he would not return to the VA stole over her.

What if he never heard about the new study being done in San Antonio? If there was one chance in a million of Rafe seeing again, Alexa wanted that chance for him. She cared, dammit!

She walked back to the horse barn. "Come on, Compadre," she said, letting the dog out. "You and I are going to find the Martinez house. I have to make sure Rafe's getting the help he needs."

The collie barked and ran in circles at the sound of Rafe's name.

CHAPTER EIGHT

ALEXA GOT DIRECTIONS to Sierra's home at the feed store where she bought supplies. The couple who owned the store had lived in the area for fifty years. They knew everyone for miles around and gave directions along the lines of "turn at the crossroad where you'll see a green dairy barn on your left. Follow that road till you can't go farther."

Like most homes in the area, the Martinez place sat at the end of a private gravel road. The compact single-story house was surrounded by undeveloped land dotted with mesquite, cottonwood and piñon trees. Alexa noticed the cottonwood had lost a majority of their bright yellow leaves, a sure sign that fall was giving way to winter.

As she pulled up in front of the house, she saw Rafe seated on a porch swing. Her pulse gave a happy kick and she scrambled out of her pickup. Holding onto Compadre's collar, she approached the wide porch, painted gray to match the house. But when she tried to speak, her voice caught in her throat.

Rafe stood up, obviously having heard the vehicle. Wood chips fluttered around his feet.

He looked fantastic in tight black jeans and a pale blue shirt that enhanced his naturally bronze skin tones. Belatedly, Alexa recognized he'd been whittling.

"Alexa?" He must have recognized her step moments before Compadre yipped excitedly and nearly bowled him over. His knife fell to the porch with a clunk. The dog head-butted Rafe's thigh, then scurried off to investigate the shiny object.

"It is me," Alexa said. "Compadre gave us away." She knelt and scooped up Rafe's knife. Fighting a desire to throw her arms around him in greeting, she straightened. "Here's your knife. I wasn't aware you were a wood-carver."

"What are you doing here?" he exclaimed. "Uh, not that I'm not glad. I am." He cleared his throat. "I fool around with carving. You caught me trying to whittle a reasonable facsimile of Dog. I'd planned to give it to you as soon as I talked Doug into driving me out to your ranch." Rafe extended a rough-hewn collie carved from a grainy wood. With the multicolored striations of the wood, the statue looked remarkably like Compadre.

Alexa ran a finger along the carving, but her hand collided with Rafe's and she snatched it back. "It's a fine likeness, Rafe. Really good."

He shrugged. "I used to carve to calm my nerves between rides at rodeos. I quit carving in boot camp. There was never time. I took it up again in Iraq while we waited to go out on missions. I made whistles and toys for local kids. I guess I'm at loose ends again. Sierra pitches a fit about my carving. She's positive I'm going to miss with the knife and cut an artery."

"Speaking of Sierra, I don't see her van. Or any vehicles. Are you here on your own?"

"She and the kids went to town for groceries. They always make a day of it. She'll pick up Curt and Chloe from school before coming home. Hey, come share my swing and tell me what brings you out this way."

"I'll, uh, take this chair. After you left, Rafe, I stewed over letting you go without my version of what happened in Houston. With my holistic practice," she added, setting her purse down and perching gingerly on a weathered deck chair. "It's probably not important to you, but I'd like to set the record straight."

Rafe felt for the swing cushion and sat back down. Compadre wagged his tail and crowded close. "Alexa, you don't have to talk about it if it's too painful."

"No, I want to. But it's…harder than I imagined to speak about even after so much time." She gulped down a shaky breath. "I…I was barely fourteen and Bobby Duval eighteen when we met. My dad hired him to be a general gofer in his office and the oil fields. If you ever saw any of the old James Dean films, that pretty much describes Bobby. Cool. Gutsy. He didn't walk. He swaggered."

Rafe scooted Compadre aside and continued to put the finishing touches on his carving. The knife dug into the soft wood, forming curls in the dog's coat. "James Dean, huh? I get the picture. You fell for each other right off."

"It wasn't that way," she said quickly. "I was

an awkward overachiever, always out of place with my peers because teachers kept jumping me ahead in school. I hated that. Neither of my parents understood I only wanted to feel normal. I graduated from college at fifteen, Rafe. My mother and my teachers were investigating medical schools for me to attend, but none would waive the age requirement for entry. Somehow mother learned I could attend osteopathic college and live at home— she didn't want me to give up my comfortable lifestyle for a college dorm." Alexa laughed, but she knew it sounded strained. "Bobby had zero advantages. He barely squeaked through high school. But he was determined to learn every aspect of the oil business from my dad. He had big dreams, and he saw right through me. I can't say why we hit it off. Bobby was a real diamond in the rough, but he just loved life and was so much fun to be around. I think he counted on me to hone his rough edges."

"I'd say you're a natural." Rafe shook off the last wood shavings from his shirt and jeans and closed his knife. He held the carving out for Alexa to take.

"Rafe, this is fantastic." She ran a finger

over the smooth wood. "It looks just like Compadre, even though you've never seen him."

"Hands-on petting," Rafe said, pocketing his knife. "Here's where I should tell you I pumped Sierra until she told me you *are* a ringer for Cameron Diaz. I'm pretty sure I know what was on your Bobby Duval's mind back then."

"You're wrong. I was geeky. Still, my mother and father weren't very happy about all the time Bobby and I spent together. They didn't want me talking to him when he delivered messages from the field. Bobby found the whole thing amusing. He considered my mom uppity but he had a grudging respect for my dad. Even before I turned nineteen and set up my office, people assumed Bobby and I were lovers. Stop!" Instinctively Alexa held up a hand. "I can tell by your smirk you're like everyone else. All Bobby and I had was a brief fling the summer I turned eighteen. And we both agreed it was a mistake."

Rafe snorted.

"I swear—it amounted to nothing."

Rafe's jaw flexed. Was he jealous? Alexa scooted closer and curved a hand over his rigid forearm. "I loved Bobby, but I wasn't *in* love with him," she stressed.

"If you say so."

"I do. Our friendship was too important to both of us to risk a romantic relationship. Besides, Bobby liked being a player. He wasn't about to commit to one woman. He was totally focused on being an oil tycoon like my dad. If he and I ever argued over anything it was that. My father was a driven man, and I knew Bobby wasn't ruthless enough. But he didn't listen. So he went from being Dad's gofer to a full-time roustabout against my advice. And Dad kept Bobby working more hours in the field so he had less time to hang out with me. That's when I studied Chinese acupuncture."

Alexa blew out a breath. This was the part she didn't like to remember. "For years Bobby nagged me to apply to medical school, so I finally relented. I was under consideration at two Texas universities, then on New Year's Eve, Bobby lost control of his Jeep during a storm. He hit a tree. A huge live oak." Alexa's voice cracked.

Rafe stopped tugging the dog's ears. "For cripe's sake, why didn't you tell Ms. Holmes she had her facts all wrong, that your friend died in a car wreck?"

"She didn't get it wrong," Alexa said tightly.

"What do you mean?"

"Bobby didn't die in the accident, Rafe. He died from complications resulting from his injuries—after he signed himself out of the hospital and came to stay with me. I begged him to go back to the hospital when he took a downturn, but he refused." Alexa couldn't believe how painful the memories still were.

"You should have hired a lawyer, Alexa."

"My dad did. A top attorney. But, the Duvals' lawyer came and said I could settle instead." Alexa closed her eyes, remembering. "I should have listened to my parents, but I just wanted it over. Bobby's parents' allegations were horrible. I thought settling would end it, but I was wrong. The media picked up the story. Reporters said I would've fought the case if I wasn't guilty of incompetence. As a result, I lost patients. Both universities passed on my med school applications. Everybody thought my moving to the ranch was taking a coward's way out…that running away suggested guilt. But…the ordeal hurt me. I...I wasn't as immune to criticism as I thought."

Rafe knew Alexa would have done everything she could for her friend, including getting him to a hospital if he'd agreed. Now he understood better why she'd been so reluctant to take him on as a patient—and so upset when their relationship had heated up.

Rafe could sympathize with Bobby. Like him, he had nothing to offer a woman like Alexa. Her folks wouldn't like his background, either. They'd think a broken-down ex-cowboy, ex-soldier wasn't good enough for their daughter. And maybe he wasn't.

Wheels spun inside Rafe's head. He'd thought maybe together they could buy and train high-quality cutting horses. There used to be a demand for them all across Texas. But, could he ask her to take on a partner—in business and life—when he couldn't even see?

"God, Alexa," was all he could manage to say.

She frowned. "I know it's bad, Rafe. But my dad said Bobby's parents wanted to ruin me and bankrupt him."

Rafe just kept shaking his head, uncertain

what to say. Alexa took his silence as criticism after she'd bared her soul to him.

She shot out of the deck chair. "Thanks for the carving, Rafe. I'll cherish it always. But… but I have to leave. Come, Compadre."

The dog licked Rafe's hand and then followed Alexa down the porch steps.

"Hey, wait," Rafe said, stirring at last. The last thing he wanted was for Alexa to go. He felt for the porch railing and used it to guide him to the steps. "Don't rush off. Stick around. In fact, stay for supper. Sierra will get after me if I let you take off before she gets home."

"Baloney! I know for a fact your sister was anything but happy about asking me to take your case."

"We had a talk about that," Rafe said. "Sierra finds it hard to stop playing big sister and mother all rolled into one. I told her I was absolutely certain Ms. Holmes didn't have her facts straight about you."

"You said that?" Alexa didn't sound completely convinced. "Thanks for the vote of confidence, Rafe. But Bobby did die on my watch. Oh, I know I did nothing to contribute to his death, but I should never have let him wheedle me into taking his case. Bobby was like family to me. I'll feel guilty about that forever."

Rafe knew all about guilt. It was a subject he'd rather not examine. "Hindsight is twenty-twenty," he settled on saying.

"I suppose. But knowing I can't change the past doesn't seem to help me quit blaming myself."

Blame? Oh, boy. There was enough of that to go around. Rafe leaned on the railing and wiped his sweaty palms down his jeans.

"Rafe, are you okay? You seem a bit, I don't know, rocky."

"I'm okay. What time is it?"

"Twenty past twelve. Can I fix you a sandwich?" Alexa offered.

"If you'll drive us to town, I'll buy you lunch."

"I'd like that, but remember I have Compadre. I can't leave him here." At least her voice sounded brighter.

"Okay, so that means we can't go to Cibolo Creek guest ranch. It's the nicest place around."

"I don't need anyplace fancy."

"I know but I wanted to take you some-where nice."

She laughed. "I appreciate the thought, but I came straight from doing chores, Rafe. I'm wearing really holey jeans."

"Okay, so let's grab tacos in town. Then we can walk around."

"My pickup is parked right in front of the bottom step."

After Rafe locked up, they headed toward her truck. Alexa opened the door for Com-padre to hop in first, then Rafe.

"I have the passenger window down," she said. "You know Compadre likes to poke his nose out. If he makes a nuisance of himself, I'll stop and tighten his doggie seat belt so he stays between us."

"You have a dog seat belt? I don't think I re-alized that when we drove to Study Butte."

"I'm a stickler. Bobby wasn't wearing his the night his Jeep hit the tree. Had he been belted in, the emergency team said his injuries wouldn't have been so bad. Now, do I turn right at the end of the lane?"

"Right…yes. Then at the first crossroad you'll turn onto highway 170."

"One-seventy follows the Rio Grande."

"We're not going that far," Rafe told her. "Lajitas is between Big Bend Park and the river. It's your typical border town. On the Mexico side is Paso Lajitas. Both towns once thrived on park visitors, then someone decided to close the airport and then closed down the border crossing. It's still heavily patrolled, but both towns went stagnant."

"What a shame."

Compadre settled his feet on Rafe's right leg and leaned out the passenger window.

"Lajitas started as an Army outpost when Pancho Villa was terrorizing the area," Rafe informed Alexa as she made the turn.

"Well, that's some claim to fame."

Rafe smiled. "I grew up on stories about Villa's raids. I always thought I'd have loved living in the west when it was woolly and untamed."

It was a moment before Alexa replied, and Rafe could almost feel her assessing him. "I can see you riding these desolate canyons hunting stray longhorns, Rafe."

"You can't see me riding with Pancho Villa's raiders?"

"Frankly, no. You'd more likely be standing with villagers, helping barricade the town against the bad guys."

Rafe knew his laughter had a darker side. "Most people around Terlingua would have seen me as one of the bad guys—a mixed-race kid. White ranchers in the area sure didn't want me dating their daughters."

"I know racism is worse in small towns. Especially border towns."

"Oh, yeah. Cattlemen have never liked sheep or sheepherders to begin with. History books won't tell you that, but it's because Mexicans and Indians introduced the sheep into south Texas. Ask any old-timer around. They're blunt about it."

"I hope times are changing for the better, Rafe."

"Me, too," he muttered, his mind flipping back to her parents.

Alexa suddenly let up on the gas. "Oh, we're here. The town is quaint, Rafe. I love the old frontier-type buildings."

"All built for tourists. You can park at this end and we can walk through town to reach Connie and Hector's shop. Or you can drive through town."

"I see a spot. Let's park here and walk."

They got out with Compadre and meandered down an uneven plank sidewalk. When Rafe tripped for about the third time, Alexa asked, "Did the military give you a prescription for a white cane, Rafe? It would help you get around better in unfamiliar places."

"No cane," he snapped. "I don't want people's pity, Alexa."

He hadn't meant to sound so harsh, but Alexa said nothing. A minute later, though, he felt her slip her arm through his.

"I know you're starving, Rafe, but slow down," she said.

"You don't have to baby me, Alexa. You know I can manage."

At his words Alexa loosened her grip a bit and he lengthened his stride.

Compadre sidled up to Rafe and he realized the dog was doing his best to keep Rafe from stumbling over the side of the raised walkway.

"I see the taco sign straight ahead," Alexa said.

Rafe dropped his arm and took her hand. "There are tables out front, and more on the side, under shade trees. If any of them are empty, let's sit there."

Hector and Connie were doing the cooking and serving as usual. "Hey," they both greeted him. "How's it going, Rafe?"

"It's going good," Rafe answered. "We'll take four courageous tacos, Connie. What would you like to drink?" Rafe turned to Alexa.

"I'm afraid to ask what a courageous taco is," she said in a low voice.

"Oh, everyone calls them that because Hector fills his tortillas too full, and you have to be courageous to eat one in public."

"Okay. I'm game. I'll take bottled water to drink. I'd also like a plain hamburger, a cooked patty if possible. For the dog."

"Sierra was here half an hour ago," Hector said. "She and the younger twins. Didn't say a word about you being in town, Rafe."

"Sierra doesn't know. Hector, Connie, this is Alexa Rob...uh, Dr. Robinson. She treated me, and dropped in for a visit after Sierra had already left."

"A doctor?" Connie sounded envious. Rafe could hear her ringing up the tacos her husband would have wrapped. "Are you thinking of moving here? We have a midwife, but that's the extent of our community medical care. For real doctoring it takes a full day to drive round-trip to Alpine. Lord help us if there's any kind of an emergency."

"I'm sorry," Alexa murmured. "I'm not an MD, and I'm just visiting."

Rafe felt her fingers tighten on his arm. He sensed Connie's query had made Alexa uncomfortable. After he paid the bill, she led them to a table. "Are you mad at me for saying you're a doctor?" he asked.

"Not mad, Rafe. I worry someone will recognize my name and connect me to those old Houston news stories."

"You're being a little paranoid, don't you think? Hard-working folks around here don't have time to focus much on outside news. And didn't it happen a while ago?"

"Um, five years ago. The story and my picture were plastered in every paper and on TV for months. And, well, you didn't see your friend's curious expression."

Rafe decided to lighten the mood. "Pretty blondes aren't the norm in Lajitas. I thought if I told them you're my doctor, it'd quell rumors I kidnapped you."

"That's ridiculous."

"Aha! I'm sure I warned you about my bad-boy reputation."

Alexa laughed. "Now you're bragging."

Rafe asked her about Esperanza and how her menagerie was faring. More than once it was on the tip of his tongue to admit he wanted to return to her ranch. But he couldn't seem to find the right opening. But then, he also needed to get his ducks in a row.

"Boy, I'm stuffed," Alexa said after they'd each polished off a second taco.

"I should have only ordered us one taco each. Sierra will kill me if we don't have room for supper."

Alexa said nothing but Rafe decided not to push. He knew Sierra would never let Alexa leave without feeding her.

"Sierra's like our mother. She loves to cook for people.

"Mmm," Alexa said noncommittally. She told him she was taking their trash to the red and white barrel that Rafe knew stood outside the taco stand. "Thanks," she called to the owners. "Those tacos were the best I've eaten in ages. Maybe ever."

"Glad you liked them," Hector said. "Come again. Rafe, bring her, you hear?"

Rafe grinned as he threaded his hands through hers for the walk back to Alexa's pickup. "You won them over."

"They're nice," she said. "It's too bad I probably won't get back this way again."

Not if he had his way, Rafe thought. But he said nothing.

WHEN ALEXA PULLED the truck in front of the house, Sierra burst out the door and flew down the steps. "Mercy, Rafe," she cried, yanking open the passenger door. "Do you have any idea how worried I've been?"

"Alexa dropped in," he said sheepishly. "I invited her to lunch, and she drove us into town. I figured we'd run into you."

"But you didn't. Next time, for pity's sake, leave me a note. Uh…hi, Dr. Robinson. Was there something you needed? We're sort of out of the way…."

Alexa got out of the truck. "I wanted to make sure Rafe knew about an interesting study I came across on the Internet."

Rafe turned to her eagerly. "Why didn't you say something before? Do you need me to come back to your ranch?"

"Uh, no. This is an experiment the military is doing in San Antonio."

Sierra caught Alexa's eye. "Come in, come in. Let's not stand around out here. The wind is kicking up."

"Sierra, I invited Alexa to stay for supper," Rafe said.

Alexa raised a hand to protest. "I don't want to put you out, Sierra. Besides, we just ate lunch."

"Of course you'll stay. We wouldn't dream of sending you out on that long drive home on an empty stomach. I'm fixing pot roast."

"We had huge tacos," Alexa and Rafe said simultaneously.

Sierra held the front door open. "Okay, then supper will be something light. Kids," she said, making shooing motions at her offspring, "take your things to your bedroom. Uncle Rafe has company and we don't want to trip on your toys."

"Let them stay," Alexa said quickly, and asked Sierra to introduce her to the children. They smiled at her tentatively but were more interested in Compadre.

Rafe had allowed the dog to follow him

in, and suddenly the gentle collie was being mauled by four excited kids.

Sierra directed Alexa to a chair across from Rafe, who sat on the sofa. "So what's this study that might interest Rafe?"

"I don't want to get your hopes up," Alexa said, leaning out to touch Rafe's knee. "But, since Ms. Holmes said you needed to keep an appointment at the VA, I think it'd be worth your time to check out what they're doing with hyperbaric recompression in San Antonio. Here, Sierra. I printed off a few paragraphs from the military hospital tip sheet." Alexa sat back, dug in her purse and passed a wrinkled page to Rafe's sister, who ran an eye over the highlighted paragraphs.

"I'm afraid this is pretty much Greek to me."

As succinctly as possible, Alexa put the experiments in laymen's terms.

"Have they actually reversed anyone's blindness?" Rafe asked.

"Not yet." Alexa bit her lip. "It's all so new," she explained.

"I'm not going to be anyone's guinea pig."

Sierra darted a worried glance at her

brother, and another at Alexa, as if urging her to convince Rafe.

Instantly Alexa pulled back. Those were the same words Bobby had thrown at her. Bobby said he was sick of being a guinea pig for his team of doctors.

Rafe drummed his knee with fidgeting fingers. "What you said sounds like science fiction. Anyway, I told Sierra I'm not fooling with the VA. I'd like to come back to your ranch, Alexa. Not as a patient," he added quickly. "As a ranch hand, if you'll have me. Or we can work a deal so I can train additional horses if you have room. I'll pay, of course." He strained toward her, as if trying to gauge her response.

Thrilled as she was by Rafe's statement, Alexa couldn't, in good conscience, agree. She wasn't going to let him pass up a chance to at least find out if VA doctors thought he'd be a good candidate for the hyperbaric studies. But before she got beyond the shock of his statement and could offer to drive him to San Antonio herself, Sierra leapt up, saying, "Rafe, you know Ms. Holmes said if you don't show up for that appointment tomorrow, you'll forfeit all of your VA benefits. That's stupid."

Rafe reared back, sputtering.

Alexa opened her mouth to intervene, but Sierra spoke again, more calmly this time. "I made arrangements with Doug's sister to keep Melina and Maris. And I promised Curt and Chloe that they could come with us. They're looking forward to visiting the Alamo while you're at the VA. You can't disappoint them."

Rafe ran a hand through his hair, apparently struggling with this decision, then acquiesced with a brief, "Okay."

Disappointed not to be taking Rafe herself, Alexa got down on her knees and admired a dollhouse Chloe dragged out to show her. "This is a wonderful dollhouse."

"My mama and daddy made it," the little girl pointed out.

Not to be outdone, Curt brought Alexa a fire truck he said his daddy had bought especially for him. Soon all four kids were laughing and playing with Alexa. One of the younger twins dragged out a box full of barnyard animals. The other dumped out a set of building blocks and asked if Alexa would help her build a barn.

Sierra had gone into the kitchen. She stuck

her head around the door frame and called, asking Rafe to join her for a minute. He got up and started across the room, heading straight through the children's toys. His foot landed on a cow that squeaked. Compadre loped over to investigate the noise and the kids stopped talking. Curt mumbled an apology and swept a path clear for his uncle.

Not wanting Rafe to feel awkward, Alexa motioned the kids to her. "Hey, let's move all this stuff out of your uncle Rafe's way. We can build a barn and corral in this corner with your blocks."

That kept everyone busy for a while, but when Rafe returned, he accidentally kicked a block under the couch. He bent down and patted the floor. In a flash Maris scrambled over, saying in a tiny voice, "I'll get it for you, Uncle Rafe." She held out the block to Rafe, who'd reclaimed his seat on the sofa.

Alexa realized the little girl wanted her uncle to play with them.

"Rafe, Maris wants to give you a block," she said. "Would you like to join us on the floor and build a roof the barn?"

He reached out to take the block, but it fell

through his fingers. It bounced and everyone watching drew in a collective breath.

Scowling, Rafe sat back and dropped his hands to his sides.

Alexa felt discouraged to see how quickly Rafe withdrew into a stony shell. She kept shooting him surreptitious glances while she and the kids finished building the corrals and populated them with plastic cows and horses. It was evident something had drastically changed since Rafe first invited her to join his family for supper.

Had he and Sierra had words over her when Rafe went to the kitchen? The children soon tired of playing with the farmyard and ran off to their room, leaving her alone with the dead-silent Rafe.

She got up from the floor and collected her purse. "You know, Rafe, I'm having second thoughts about staying. I'll stop by the kitchen and tell Sierra I'd really rather not drive home after dark."

He stood up right away. "I'll tell her. It has gotten late." He began herding Alexa toward the front door as if he couldn't wait to see the last of her.

Pausing at the threshold long enough to call

Compadre, Alexa shifted from foot to foot, and finally stepped outside. "Rafe, I wish you the best of luck at the VA. Make sure you ask them about the possibility of getting into that hyperbaric study."

"I'll think about it. Thanks."

"I'll see you later?" Alexa tossed the question out carelessly, doing her best to sound upbeat.

Rafe made some noncommittal sound, and as Alexa drove away, she wondered what had caused his mood to change. And whether this might be the last time she would ever see him.

CHAPTER NINE

RAFE SAT ON A WOODEN bench anchored outside the sprawling VA facility in San Antonio where he'd agreed to meet Sierra after his appointment. The squeal of her slipping fan belt told him she'd arrived. It was time she got that fixed. As he stood, it crossed his mind that when she did, he wouldn't know her vehicle from any other.

"Sorry we're late." Sierra sounded breathless as she came around the van to assist him into the front seat.

"Sierra, I can get in a damned car on my own," Rafe said. He heard Curt and Chloe chattering in the far back and recognized the sound of turning pages. "Hi, Uncle Rafe. Mama bought Chloe and me a neat picture book of the Alamo. It's a cool place."

"Yeah?" Rafe buckled his seat belt.

"Since you bit my head off, I assume your appointment didn't go well, Rafe." Sierra climbed in the van, but didn't pull away from the curb right away.

"It went fine." He closed his eyes.

"I see they took blood."

He tore off the tape from his arm, then stuffed it into the trash bag Sierra kept in the van.

"I have to stop at the gate to turn in this visitor pass," Sierra said. Once she'd done that, she took a sharp right turn to exit the VA grounds. "Did you ask about the study Alexa told us about?"

"The doctor said I'm not a good candidate."

"The guy sees you once and he knows that?" Sierra said grumpily. "Is he a doctor who works directly with the program?"

"Let it go, Sierra. An ophthalmologist and a neurologist poked and prodded me. Both had my history. Neither found anything new. They can't explain why I can see wavy gray outlines. But I'm never going to wake up one day and miraculously have my sight again."

"You're bummed. But two doctors can't know everything, Rafe. New discoveries are made every day. Maybe things will be different at your next visit."

"There is no next visit. End of discussion." Rafe shoved a disc into the player. It was Toby Keith. Crossing his arms, he settled back for the ride home.

They arrived after dark. Doug had picked up Maris and Melina from his sister's and had already given them supper.

"I'll warm up leftovers," Sierra told Rafe. "I smell spaghetti and garlic bread."

"I'm not hungry." Rafe shook out the blankets to make his bed on the couch.

"You need to…" Doug started, but Sierra silenced him.

"Doug will you put Chloe and Curt to bed?"

Rafe heard them kiss, and Doug said, "Pour me a glass of milk, Sierra. I'll join you later in the kitchen."

Rafe didn't go right to sleep. He lay awake listening to the low rise and fall of his sister and brother-in-law's voices. He couldn't distinguish what they said, but had little doubt that he was the topic of their conversation. He didn't care. He didn't frigging care about anything.

That attitude prevailed in the days following his appointment. Before Alexa's surprise visit and the trip to San Antonio, he'd pestered Doug to take him back to Alexa's. After the appointment, days rolled into weeks, during which time he didn't mention it. Nor did he bring up Alexa's name.

By December, he was downright surly all day, everyday. Rafe knew Sierra was ready to toss him out on his keister.

At supper one evening, she filled his plate with meatloaf and mashed potatoes and smacked it down in front of him. "Rafe, you've been bad tempered long enough. Things have to change."

He pushed his plate aside and started to get up from the table.

"No, you sit back down," Sierra commanded in a voice that made her kids fall silent. "You've moped long enough. You haven't whittled in ages. The way I see it, you're back at square one. Back to where we all tiptoed circles around you. Living with this tension isn't good for anyone. Talk, Rafe! Doug and I can't help you if we don't know what's wrong."

"Isn't that obvious? I can't see more than grainy shadows. I've broken a plate and three glasses, and crushed Chloe's favorite Barbie doll."

"We know," Sierra said gently. "But, if you won't return to the VA and look for a cure, you'll have to learn to live as you are."

"What am I doing if not living?"

"You're existing. You're back to doing nothing like you did before you saw Alexa. You know I'd do anything to help you, Rafe. But I honestly don't know what else I *can* do."

"I was busier at Alexa's, " Rafe blurted. "I felt more like my old self. I was…" He stopped abruptly, partway out of his chair.

Sierra grabbed Rafe's hand. "Say it, Rafe. It won't hurt my feelings. You were happier at Alexa's."

"Yeah," he finally admitted. "I want to go back. I told you before. But she doesn't need a washed-up blind guy hanging around, keeping her from a normal life."

Sierra yanked his hand so hard Rafe had no choice but to sit again. He steeled himself for his sister's lecture. "If you've finished your pity party, eat while the food's warm."

Oddly, it was Doug who took Rafe to task next. His brother-in-law had always seemed like a secret ally. "Look, Rafe, you have your full mental faculties and all your limbs intact. Plenty of your fellow soldiers are worse off. I saw a documentary the other day about a dude who'd lost both legs who just ran in a marathon."

"That's true," Sierra vouched.

Throughout the meal, Rafe pondered what to do. "What's on your agenda tomorrow, Doug?" he asked, once the kids had trooped off to take baths. "I was hoping you could drive me to Alexa's. You can just drop me at her gate and go."

"Did you two have a fight last month when she visited?" Sierra asked worriedly. "I think Doug should stick around until you have a chance to speak with her."

"We didn't fight, exactly. I just had a lot of doubts and made it easy for Alexa to leave. I'll have some explaining to do. If Doug hangs around, Alexa will see him as an excuse not to listen to me."

"Can do," Doug said. "But, so you know, Rafe, our door is always open to you. The addition will be finished by spring. If you need a permanent spot, we'll be more than happy to accommodate you. We just don't like seeing you fritter your life away."

"I know." Rafe slapped Doug's back and Doug did the same in return. Then Rafe rounded the table and hugged Sierra.

"I love you, Rafe," she snuffled. "I just want to see you happy."

"I know," he said. "Believe me, I've needed your love."

THE NEXT DAY, on the drive to Alexa's, Rafe and Doug discussed Doug's job. "In spite of all our efforts," Doug said, "our border remains porous as hell. Last month, ranches near Terlingua reported cows butchered where border crossers camped out. Feel free to use that info to convince Alexa to hire you. I'm not worried about the families who cross, but the men they get as guides are thugs. Especially those who mule drugs. A woman living alone is an easy mark for looters, or worse."

"Alexa's got guts. And let's face it, Doug, what can I offer her in the way of backup?"

"More than you think. To anyone keeping tabs on her ranch, you look like a strong hired hand."

Rafe nodded. That made him feel marginally better. He would use it to convince Alexa.

They turned onto her dirt road and Doug slowed. "I think that's her by the barn," he said when they stopped at the gate. "She's unloading a pickup filled with hay bales. I'll say this much for your doctor, she doesn't shy from hard work."

"Don't call her my doctor, Doug. I hope you can soon call her my partner. I'm considering trying to invest in her operation. Together we could train horses."

"Well, good luck." Doug stopped at the gate and let his SUV idle. "Like Sierra said, I can spare the time if you want me to wait."

"Thanks. But clearing the air is likely to be a lengthy process. I'm banking it'll go easier if Alexa has no way to kick me out."

Doug laughed as Rafe opened the passenger door. He passed Rafe his duffel. "Whatever happens, and my money's on you, phone Sierra. She'll worry till you do."

Rafe nodded before shutting the SUV door. He didn't move until he heard Doug drive off, and then he made his way to the porch by the kitchen door. He had no idea if Alexa had witnessed his arrival, but he felt better the minute Dog trotted up. The collie gave a few happy yips and nudged his furry head against Rafe's hand.

Dropping his duffel on the porch, Rafe let the collie lead him to Alexa. By the time they reached the front of her pickup, she still hadn't said a word.

"Alexa?" he called, unsure exactly where she stood. She had to be nearby, because he could hear her huffing and he made out the thump of hay bales being tossed into the barn. Clearing his throat, he called out more loudly.

"Rafe?" Alexa sounded genuinely shocked to see him. "Sorry, I was listening to music on my iPod. How on earth did you get here?"

"Doug dropped me off. He's headed to his patrol."

"Really? Well, I thought you must've fallen off the face of the earth. I haven't heard boo from you in over a month. But, who's counting?"

Rafe heard her strip off her gloves and slap them against her palm. He also hadn't missed the testiness in her words. "I should've called. But, I had a lot of thinking to do."

"Oh? Are you being considered for the study?"

"Alexa, I had to come back. This is one of the few places where I can really breathe."

He realized he hadn't answered her question. She wouldn't like him being evasive. At least Compadre was happy to have him back.

"Do you think you can just pop in without warning?" she asked.

"No. I...hoped for starters you'd let me continue training Esperanza." Rafe decided this was not the time to mention the possibility of being partners. "Well, I'll even feed your goats."

HE HATED THE GOATS. Alexa took a closer look at Rafe. His eyes were dull, and his face more gaunt than she remembered. If he'd come back full of spit and vinegar, she would have turned him away without a thought. After all, he'd practically thrown her out of Sierra's the last time they'd been together. Maybe that's what made him uncertain about her reaction. As much as she'd like to say yes, she waffled. "I've got lots to do to prepare the ranch for winter." It was the same excuse she'd given her mother for staying home instead of traveling to Houston for Thanksgiving. Really she'd moped about, hoping to hear from Rafe.

"I can help," he said, sounding eager.

"Well, the horses are getting shortchanged. Jim Buckley still wants Esperanza for his daughter. He came by last week, and was pleased with all you'd done with her."

"Great! So, is that a yes I can stay, or a maybe?" The news about Buckley obviously bolstered Rafe's ego.

She eased out a rough sigh. "I suppose we can try it for a while."

Was he hiding a smile? Alexa wondered. "Shall I go stow my duffel in the room I had before?" he asked.

"It's as you left it. Compadre, go with Rafe." Alexa gave the dog a hand signal he understood and the two took off. Instead of going straight back to unloading bales, Alexa narrowed her eyes and stared after the retreating pair. What had gone on at Sierra's, or the VA, she wondered? Rafe was acting so contrite. But he walked with the old confidence. She sighed and decided to let him talk in his own time. Donning her gloves, she threw her muscle into emptying the pickup.

IT TOOK THE REST OF THAT week for Alexa to get back into the work routine she and Rafe had established before he left. Erratic storms forced them to spend more time indoors, and Rafe carved endless animals.

She swept up the piles of shavings herself. Although Rafe spoke with her as they went about their day, she sensed something was bothering him and was reluctant to push him in any way.

Alexa took advantage of their time indoors to mix potions from her dried herbs and pour candles for the winter months. She also canned the last fruit she bought at the store. As the week progressed, she noticed Rafe did more aimless pacing. She sealed a final jar of pears, and then washed up.

"Rafe, we can go to the hot springs even in the rain. It's covered and I have umbrellas for the walk there."

"No," he said, clearly testy.

Alexa noticed he hadn't brought up the subject of additional treatments. She wondered why. "Last night I mixed a new batch of oil with patchouli and sandalwood, guaranteed to relax you. Or, are you interested in trying another acupuncture treatment?"

"I'm not here for doctoring, Alexa. I guess I didn't make that clear enough." He fidgeted, looking uncomfortable. "I...ah, had in mind to invest in your horse training operation. I was thinking maybe we could expand into the quarter horse trade."

That stunned Alexa. He didn't want any more treatments from her? Maybe his visit to the VA had convinced him Ms. Holmes had spoken the truth after all. A pain stabbed through her.

"Why would you think I need a business partner?" she said curtly. "In case you hadn't noticed, I get along fine on my own. It looks as if the rain's let up. I'm going out to release the great horned owl."

She walked over to get her rubber boots and a raincoat, and Rafe followed her, putting a hand on the door so she couldn't leave. "Alexa, I don't want you to be my doctor."

He'd made that clear already. "I understood that. Now let go of the door. I said I'm going to release the owl."

"Another owl? I thought you let the big one go the day Sierra came and brought that Holmes woman from the VA."

"Same owl." Alexa would be darned if she'd

admit to Rafe that his leaving had shaken her faith in herself and her ability to heal. "It was too early then. He's a beautiful, gentle creature. I needed to be absolutely sure he can hunt on his own, but I have to do this now—before really bad weather sets in."

"Can I tag along?" Rafe shrugged into the raincoat he'd brought with him, the kind cowboys wore with a split up the back for riding in the rain.

His company was the last thing Alexa wanted, but it would be downright mean to tell him that. However, she didn't have it in her to be mean just because he didn't trust her to doctor him. "Remember, Compadre has to stay here. Owls are nervous creatures so you'll have to keep back until I see if he makes the effort to hunt."

"How will you do that?"

"I have some field mice I bought for this purpose."

"You're sacrificing defenseless field mice?" Alexa knew he was teasing by the grin on his face.

She jabbed his ribs with a sharp elbow, a little harder than she'd intended.

"Hey, I was kidding, okay?"

Inside the small barn, she carried the owl's cage to the door. "Weeks ago I removed his wing splint. Oh, aren't you the most beautiful bird," she crooned, still reluctant to open the cage. "What if he hasn't mended well enough to survive on his own?" she muttered.

"Softie," Rafe teased. "You can speculate forever, Alexa. You won't know for certain if his wing is healed until you open that cage door and watch him fly away."

"It's time." The night air felt thick with the increased humidity as they walked outside.

RAFE FINALLY HEARD the creak of the cage door. His cheeks were fanned by a rush of air as the bird lifted off. Rafe didn't stay back but moved in behind Alexa and put his hands on her shoulders to steady her because he couldn't miss the catch in her throat

"He flew up into a tall cedar," Alexa told him. "Okay, it's time to release the field mice." She grabbed a small cage. "I always give them a fighting chance to hide. There they go! Uh-oh, I think he spotted his food. No, I can't tell where he went. The clouds dropped. I can't see him," Alexa said plaintively.

Rafe turned her and pulled her against his chest. She was still holding the cage and it banged his hip, but he didn't care. "Do you see any movement?" he asked her, feeling her lift her head. In the night gloom he couldn't make out any shapes.

"I'm afraid it's gotten too dark," Alexa said unhappily.

"Why didn't you wait and release him in the morning?"

"This is an owl's prime time to hunt. They see best in the dark."

"Unlike me," Rafe quipped, hoping to break the tension.

"Rafe, I'm sorry. I know you live day and night in the dark."

"It's okay." He raked a kiss across Alexa's hair. "I never want you to hold back saying anything on my account. It's bad to keep things bottled up. I know—I speak from experience."

"You mean because you don't talk about the war?"

"Partly. I meant…" He seemed to scrabble for words.

Alexa locked the barn then came back to stand beside him. "If you don't trust me with your insecurities, that's okay, Rafe. But you should talk to someone. I can truthfully say I felt better after I told you about my ordeal with Bobby and his parents."

As they started toward the house, Rafe slipped an arm around Alexa's waist. "I know that wasn't easy, Alexa. When I think about losing my friends Joey and Mike, something inside me shuts down."

"Believe me, I hear you. Bobby was my very best friend, remember."

It was time for Rafe to unburden his conscience. "People say I'm a hero, Alexa, but I didn't act like one with Mike and Joey."

"I know that's bogus," she said. "I read the reports from your men. You did everything you could to save as many of them as possible."

"I'm not sure about that, but I've been a coward since I've come back. Their folks practically adopted me. Mike's mom asked to visit me when I got Stateside but I refused. I couldn't face her, Alexa. Or Joey's parents and his wife. Joey's mom wrote me a letter. I had a nurse return it unopened. If that doesn't make me lily-livered, what does?"

"It makes you human," Alexa said, squeezing his hand and laying her head lightly on his shoulder. "But, one day, for your own sake, you do need to talk to them."

"I've thought a zillion times about asking Sierra to take me down there. If nothing else, they probably need to know if the account the army gave them was true. Alexa, you said Bobby's parents blamed you for his death. I'm not sure I could handle it if Joey and Mike's families think I didn't do enough. Maybe they'll resent me for not dying."

"Rafe, no parent would think that. Bobby's folks never liked me. I'm sure your friends' parents just need closure. So do you." She paused at the kitchen door. "It's a huge step, Rafe, but if you want, I'll drive you to Terlingua anytime. Catch your back."

"I should go," he mumbled as she opened the door and Compadre charged out. "If I leave loose ends I'll never move forward with my life. The neurologist made that point on my last VA visit."

"This is one hurdle I'd be glad to help with, Rafe."

He had to act fast before he had second thoughts. "Can we go tomorrow?"

"I'd be honored, Rafe. We can leave right after I feed the animals."

"It's going to be one of the hardest things I've ever done," he admitted. "I'll probably try to back out, Alexa. Don't let me."

"If you back out you'll have to feed the goats."

Rafe let a minute tick past. Compadre trotted back and they all went inside. "I thought maybe you hadn't noticed. Nothing gets by you, I guess."

"I know the smell of goats takes you back to a place you'd rather forget. That's a head issue, Rafe. Visiting Mike and Joey's families is an issue of the heart—a whole different matter. Although, come to think of it, I'm not great at dealing with either."

Rafe wondered if she was still talking about Bobby. Sobered, he took Dog and went to get ready for bed. How would Alexa react if he told her the reason he had to face his friend's families and rid his heart of pain was so he could make room to love her? One thing at a time. But, he'd have to get around to that soon.

THE SUN CAME AND WENT behind fast moving clouds on the drive to Terlingua. The nearer they got to Rafe's childhood town, the more nervous he grew. He kept rubbing his sweaty hands over his denim-clad thighs.

"You're going to wear out the fabric of your jeans, Rafe," Alexa said.

She didn't miss a thing, Rafe thought, ducking his chin to avoid Compadre's wet tongue.

"Even the dog knows you're upset today, Rafe. Hey, we're at the address you gave me for Mike Herrera's parents. There's a car in the carport." Alexa pulled her pickup into the driveway then turned to straighten Rafe's collar. "I don't mind going in with you," she said quietly.

"I'd appreciate that," Rafe said, trying to calm the quaking that seemed to be overtaking his big frame.

But his fears were unfounded. He knew Mike's mother was a short round woman with dark eyes and dark hair, and when she opened the door, she grabbed him close, smothering him in hugs, her tears dampening his shirt. "The army told Big Mike and me you'd lost your sight, Rafe. We knew you must be having a tough time when you didn't come to Mike or Joey's funerals. I tried to visit you once, but they turned me away."

Rafe's throat tightened and he couldn't speak, but Alexa took over for him. "We brought small flags to place on the men's graves, Mrs. Herrera. I'm Alexa Robinson, by the way."

"Oh…Alexa, I can't thank you enough for bringing Rafe all this way."

"It was Rafe's idea, totally," Alexa injected.

The woman held on to Rafe. "Your unit's colonel gave us Mike's medal. He told us what a terrible ambush you all got caught in. Last time Mike was home on leave, all he could talk about was how you three finally got to be together. Mike loved being a jeep gunner. He said he couldn't ever come back to live in Terlingua. His dad and I felt he was saying goodbye one way or another. That's why I tried to see you. I…wanted you to know that, Rafe."

"Thanks, Mama Herrera." Rafe enveloped the stout woman in a bear hug. "Nothing has hurt me more than losing Mike and Joey." Tears spilled down his face. "God, I would have changed places with them in a heart-beat."

"I know that. So do the Verdugos. Don't know if anyone's told you Joey's wife had a baby girl after Joey died. The two of them live with Chuck and Marta. In a lot of ways that's made it easier for them to bear Joey's loss, but…"

Rafe could tell by her voice that she couldn't continue. "Joey flashed around pictures of his wife," he said. "He was crazy in love. I can't believe he didn't brag about being a dad."

"Joey never knew, but I should let them tell you. Getting in touch was harder from Afghanistan than when you boys were in Iraq. When the army gave Maci Ann Joey's personal effects, there were two unopened letters that she'd written to tell him the news. They both arrived at your base camp after you left to go on that last patrol."

"How sad," Alexa murmured, hurriedly taking Rafe's hand. "Mrs. Herrera, we hate to make this such a quick visit, but we need to stop at the Verdugos and still have time to run by the cemetery, then get back to the Big Bend area before the weather turns bad."

Rafe couldn't believe Joey hadn't known he

was going to be a dad. He knew Alexa had picked up on his grief and had stepped in to bail him out yet again.

Mike's mom hugged Rafe one last time. "You drive careful, hear? And if you get down this way again, plan to stay longer. Come back when Big Mike's home. You boys spent so much time together, having you survive is like getting lucky with one of three sons."

Rafe blinked hard all the way to the Verdugos. There the scene was pretty much a repeat of Mrs. Herrera's effusive welcome. Only Maci Ann Verdugo, Joey's wife, asked the hard questions. "Why were Joey and Mike killed by the first rocket blast if you were their leader?"

"They volunteered to ride point," Rafe explained. "They did that a lot. It's like asking why Joey rode bulls. He sought out danger. As their ranking officer, I brought up the rear in the last Humvee. The front of our patrol had rounded a bend. I…got there too late…." Every ounce of Rafe's regrets hung heavily in the air.

Joey's mother, holding her granddaughter, deftly led Rafe and Alexa out of the house. "Rafe, I hope you excuse Maci Ann. She doesn't know you like we do. She also feels guilty for not reaching Joey as soon as she learned she was pregnant."

"I understand, Marta. I swear if I could turn back the clock on that day, I would."

"I know, Rafe. And heaven can see you've got trouble of your own. We feel blessed to have our sweet little Jolie. You can't see her, Rafe, but she's the spitting image of her daddy at the same age."

A gust of wind skittered oak leaves across the sidewalk, the sound making Rafe uneasy. Once again Alexa seemed to pick up on his mood.

"Mrs. Verdugo," she said. "Rafe and I are going to put out flags at the cemetery. Please make clear to Maci Ann that Mike and Joey were like Rafe's brothers. He lost his best friends that day."

Joey's mother patted Rafe's cheek. "Lordy, I know that. You take care of this one." She leaned closer to Alexa. "Many a day I've thought the one left behind has it the hardest."

At the cemetery, Rafe knelt at each grave. He wept, and Alexa wept watching him. As they headed home, the sky opened and rain poured down as if in sympathy. Both Alexa and Rafe said little, lost in their own thoughts.

"They're nice people," Rafe said as Alexa turned onto the winding road that led to her ranch. "Thank you for taking me," he added. "It was a long-overdue trip. Cathartic."

"You're welcome. I'm proud of you, Rafe. Most people aren't aware that sometimes living is tougher than dying. Mrs. Herrera and Mrs. Verdugo know that."

"Not Joey's wife."

"She's young. It'll take her time to heal."

"It must be tough being a young widow," Rafe said sadly. "With a baby to raise alone."

"Not alone. Her baby has doting grandparents. She's luckier than many."

Rafe ran a restless hand over Compadre's curly coat and drifted back into silence.

"WE'RE HOME," ALEXA announced around a sigh. "You go on in. I need to check the animals. There's been lightning off in the distance and I hear the first roll of thunder. These electric storms affect the wild animals more than the horses. It's their instinct to burrow in and they can't do that in cages."

"I get antsy, too," Rafe admitted. "I want to help, Alexa."

They did their best to settle the animals by covering their cages and dashed back inside the house seconds ahead of the rain.

A flash of lightning lit an otherwise black kitchen and Alexa clicked the light switch a few times. "Darn, the power's out." She was breathing hard and so was Rafe. In a way, the storm was a fitting end to a tough day.

"Hey, the darkness puts us on equal footing," Rafe said, teasing as he angled Alexa's face up to his.

Alexa felt as if the lightning had followed them inside. Her stomach quivered, and her heart felt electrified as his thumbs stroked back and forth across her cheekbones.

"I can't find words for what I feel, Alexa," he said. "Uplifted. Humbled."

"I understand." She ran her hands up and over Rafe's wide shoulders. That's when it really dawned on her. "Rafe, I don't want to be your doctor now."

Rafe took her words as an invitation, the way Alexa hoped he would, and tugged her tighter against him. Their lips met and brushed several times, then as if equally desperate, they clung to each other, giving and seeking comfort. The thunder rolled noisily overhead. Lightning flashed. But inside the kitchen their focus narrowed to just the two of them and their mutual needs. Urgency grew and in unspoken agreement they left a hasty trail of discarded clothing from the kitchen into Alexa's bedroom.

Rafe's fingers trailed a hot path along Alexa's bare skin. The more he touched her, the more she wanted to be touched. Touched and explored. It had been so very long since she'd felt a loving touch.

Somehow they made their way into her bed in pitch darkness. Following Rafe's lead, Alexa reveled in the tautness of his smooth back, the long lines of muscle that hardened under the barest scrape of her palms across his flesh. At some point it struck her—Rafe had been right. In her unlit bedroom, they were equals, though he was more adept at finding every one of her sweet spots. Oh, yes, Rafe knew his way around a woman's body. He knew how to make her feel cherished. Alexa suddenly remembered protection. Pushing weakly against Rafe's shoulders, she tipped her head back a fraction. "Rafe."

He stopped suckling her breast and groaned. Setting two fingers on her lips, he said in a gravelly, intense voice, "I swear, Alexa, if you're about to bring up the doctor-patient relationship again...just, don't."

"Protection, Rafe." Her voice sounded husky to her own ears. "In my office next door—I have an unopened box of condoms. They were in a kit I ordered when I considered doing volunteer work." Her explanation sounded a little ragged since she spoke against the delicious tickle of Rafe's mouth. But he stirred and leaned up on an elbow.

"You'd better bring the whole box, Alexa. The night is young."

She stumbled into her office and yanked open three cabinets before she found the box. She ripped off the plastic and grabbed a handful of condoms then hurried back to bed.

Their first time making love couldn't have been more perfectly choreographed. They didn't need to talk. They didn't need to see. They lost themselves in feeling. In experiencing each other.

Rafe was a generous lover and made Alexa

feel bold. Strong. Adored. Hours later she smiled as she lay awake with his head pillowed on her shoulder. Faint streaks of dawn flickered between the curtains. Alexa stretched. The storm inside and out had passed at least momentarily, and Rafe slept peacefully. She scooted up a bit so she could watch the flutter of his long, dark eyelashes against the high curve of his cheeks. She toyed with the thick black strands of his hair, concerned that the *L* word might have slipped from her lips more than once during the height of passion. She didn't want him worrying that she was rushing things. She wasn't. She was content with the moment.

Alexa hated to leave the warmth of the bed and the security she felt in the weight of his arm curved around her middle, but nature called. She went to the bathroom down the hall so as not to disturb Rafe. A glance in the mirror revealed she looked a mess, so she showered quickly and used the peach cream Rafe seemed to like. On returning to her room, she was surprised and disappointed to find the bed empty. He'd taken his clothes, even. The only evidence this hadn't been another dream were the tangled sheets and a dented second pillow.

She threw on some clothes and went to look for Rafe. Compadre beat her to his room. He pawed at the closed door. Alexa heard Rafe's shower running and tried the doorknob, but it was locked. "Come on, Compadre. Rafe wants his privacy. I'll switch on the alternate power generator, and surprise him with cinnamon French toast."

She hummed as she beat the eggs. Soon the whole house smelled of vanilla and cinnamon.

Rafe emerged from his room, but didn't take a seat at the table. "Look, Alexa, I came to apologize for taking advantage of your sympathy last night."

"What?" She turned from the stove, not liking the harsh set of his mouth, which had felt so soft and pliant on hers. But hadn't she feared he might read too much into her feelings? Still, anger bubbled up. "Are you accusing me of having pity sex? That's a load of crap, Rafe."

"Honesty is my new policy, remember? And I can tell from your mood this romance thing's not working."

"Oh, all I can tell is that you're a complete jerk. You won't admit what you want or need. Fix your own darned breakfast." She dumped his favorite meal in the trash.

Her heart, which had felt buoyant earlier, now sat heavy as lead in her chest. All his crawling back, making noise about being able to breathe here, and that big talk about wanting them to be partners—it was lies. The only thing Rafe Eaglefeather wanted was a simple roll in the hay.

At least her animals needed her. Alexa yanked on her boots, jacket and gloves and stormed out to the barn.

CHAPTER TEN

RAFE LEANED ON THE KITCHEN sink for a long time, staring out the window, willing his eyes to see more than murky shadows. He wanted to be the man he used to be for Alexa. A whole man.

God, but he'd hated discovering it was a lie when he told Alexa they were on equal footing in her dark bedroom. How many damned condoms had he dropped before she brushed his fumbling efforts aside and took charge of opening a packet? He'd explored every delicate feature on her face, yet had no right to tell her he found her beautiful, because he couldn't see her.

Maybe this morning, as she lingered in the afterglow of satisfaction, she didn't think his ineptness was a big deal. But, he knew it would surely surface sometime in the future. When he woke to find Alexa had vanished, and had no damned idea where she'd gone, he knew he'd never be on equal footing with Alexa. She must know it, too. Why else had she hesitated to answer when he said he wanted to be a partner in her horse business? All she wanted to talk about was his emotional, roller-coaster day, and how he must feel as if a burden had been lifted from him to have finally seen Mrs. Herrera, Mrs. Verdugo and Joey's wife. But he hadn't *seen* them, and that was the issue. Nor had he seen Alexa when they finally made love. No, the burden of his blindness was still there, and it left him feeling like half a man.

Last night had only come about because Alexa felt sorry for him. Sympathy and pity. To Rafe, they were one and the same. Had he even remembered protection? No. Luckily Alexa had. Getting her pregnant would have screwed up her life. His, too, he supposed. Marriage. Fatherhood. Scary steps for even men with twenty-twenty eyesight. The hell of it was, he loved Alexa and wanted to spend his life with her. But it wouldn't be fair to her.

He heard Dog scratching at the back door. "You need to go out?" He opened the door and realized once again how attached he'd gotten to Alexa's pet. She'd even accused him of stealing the collie's affection.

Everything was muddled in his mind. Should he go back to Doug and Sierra's? The idea of running away again left a bad taste in his mouth. Maybe he and Alexa could strike some kind of a deal where he could still help with the horses but would fix up the tack room in the barn and live there.

Rafe grabbed his slicker and headed for the door. Compadre wasn't on the porch, which meant he was with Alexa, and Rafe would have to navigate alone. Maybe he should get a white cane. The very notion depressed him. He could also stop being so stubborn and go back to the VA. Like Sierra said, why take one doctor's word about that hyperbaric study? Another option was to rent an apartment in San Antonio and let the VA teach him how to live with blindness.

Bad plan. He felt claustrophobic just crossing the threshold at the clinic. And he couldn't imagine living days on end cooped up in an efficiency apartment.

A phone rang, and the ring tone identified it as Alexa's cell. The tune kept playing, so Rafe turned back into the kitchen and groped for it on the counter. Fumbling it open, he said a breathless "Hello."

"Who is this?" A snippy woman imperiously demanded to know if she'd reached the number for Alexa Robinson.

The woman sounded so cold, Rafe felt like telling the caller she'd reached a wrong number. But Alexa didn't receive many calls. This could be important.

"Alexa's outside. If you'd care to hold, I can get her."

"Who, pray tell, are you? And why are you answering my daughter's phone?"

Oh, shit! Alexa's mother. The last time the woman called while Rafe was here, Alexa had pointedly neglected to mention her boarder. Obviously she still hadn't said anything to her mother, but Rafe wasn't about to explain. "Hold on, Mrs. Robinson, I'll find Alexa." Dashing out, he aimed for the barn. He took the phone away from his ear again, but he could still hear Alexa's mother reeling off questions, and she didn't sound happy at being ignored.

"Alexa," Rafe yelled. The scrape of metal on metal indicated she'd exited the chicken pen. "Phone," he said.

"A call?" She stepped directly into Rafe's fuzzy vision. "Who is it? I didn't realize I'd come out without my phone." She took the cell phone from Rafe and said hello, then expelled a noisy breath.

"Mother, calm down. I did neglect to mention I have someone helping me train horses. Who? An ex-G.I. But he's very experienced. He worked with rodeo stock prior to being in the army."

Rafe toyed with getting out of there, but as if Alexa read his mind, she reached out and shackled his wrist.

"It slipped my mind, Mother. Uh, he came in October. Yes, I know I've talked to you and Dad several times since. He's not a rodeo bum. For your information he's a war hero. No, you don't need to fly down here."

Rafe squeezed the bridge of his nose. Boy, the wobble in Alexa's voice made her sound insecure. And if the squeaks coming from the phone were any indication, her mother was laying the guilt on thick.

"I wasn't handing you excuses about not coming home for Thanksgiving. I have animals. Rafe wasn't here, and anyway, his responsibilities don't extend to caring for my wildlife. Rafe Eaglefeather. Tell Daddy to look up his rodeo stats. He was a grand champion bronc rider. Yes, he lives in the house. You know there isn't a bunkhouse, Mother. What? Only animals live in barns." She hauled in a deep breath. "We'll have to finish this later, after we both calm down. Goodbye." Alexa shut the phone and shoved it in her jeans pocket, still gripping Rafe's wrist. "Rafe, what possessed you to answer my mother's call?"

"I thought it might be important. And how in hell would I know it was your mother? You know I can't see the call display."

Alexa sighed. "I swear I can tell by her ring. It bleats guilt, guilt, guilt. Anytime Mother phones…oh, just forget it. She doesn't trust me to act grown up."

"I didn't mean to cause problems for you…" Rafe broke off at the sound of a vehicle pulling in beside the corral. "That engine sounds like a Humvee," he said.

"It is a Hummer. Jim Buckley. He's the one who's considering buying Esperanza for his daughter. He bought a gelding from me two years ago for his son. A great pinto." Releasing Rafe's hand, Alexa walked away from him.

Unsure if he should follow or return to the house, Rafe dropped a hand to Dog's head. It was evident the collie would rather tag along after Alexa. When it started to drizzle, Rafe decided to go on back to the house. He'd barely taken a step in that direction when Alexa called to him.

"Rafe? Do you mind bringing Esperanza out into the corral? Mr. Buckley's wife asked him to take a second look at two horses before they buy. I'll roll the barrels out, and you can run her around them."

Proud of the horse he'd helped train, Rafe headed for the mare's stall and passed a fast brush over her coat to make her shine. "Strut your stuff, girl. You're as ready to be a winning barrel racer as any horse out there," he said, stroking her neck as he clipped a lead rope to her halter.

The corral was tacky with mud. Rafe hoped, for Alexa's sake, that the horse would perform well in these conditions. After all, selling horses was her business.

He let out the rope and with a whinny Esperanza went straight into tight, running turns in and out around the barrels. On the third pass, Rafe heard the man say, "She's a beauty, Alexa. She's the one I want. I'll give you half her fee now, and the rest on delivery. I would have brought a trailer today, but my wife is bent on keeping it a secret until Devon's birthday tomorrow. You said delivery poses no problem."

"Morning or afternoon?"

"Midday's best. We traditionally fix a birthday lunch, and serve cake and ice cream before either of our kids get to open their gifts."

"Rafe, would you bring Esperanza over so Jim can take a closer look. I'll run to my office and bring her health certificates and breeding papers. She's not pedigreed, Jim, but she comes from a good farm and had a good sire, like I said before."

"I'm impressed with her smooth gait," Jim said. "My daughter turns twelve tomorrow. I think they'll make a good match."

The man seemed to hesitate, and Rafe realized he must have extended his hand for him to shake.

"Alexa said last time I stopped by that you'd trained the mare. She said you were ex-army, but that you used to rodeo. She didn't tell me you trained this horse without being able to see. That's doubly impressive. Devon will be good to her."

"Is your daughter an experienced rider?" Rafe asked.

"I run cattle. Devon's ridden since she could climb into a saddle. She's determined to take up junior barrel racing. My wife's anxious, so I promised her I'd find the best, smartest, most gentle horse available."

"Esperanza is all of that." Rafe hooked an arm over the mare's neck. "At first she didn't like the scent of Alexa's wild animals, but lately, she doesn't bat an ear."

ALEXA JOINED THEM once more. "The mountain cats are gone so that helped. I don't have to tell you, Jim, a well-trained horse can get feisty around predators."

Rafe laughed. "I'll attest to that. I recently got tossed off one of Alexa's saddle horses when we met a pack of hungry coyotes."

Alexa felt she needed to defend Rafe. "I got Compadre's rope tangled around your gelding's feet," she said.

Jim thumbed back his Stetson. "It's something that you ride, Rafe. So, you have partial vision, then?"

"Nothing to speak of. A few outlines. And that's thanks to Alexa's acupuncture. I can find my way around a kitchen well enough now so I shouldn't starve."

It made Alexa uneasy to hear Rafe mention her treatments, especially since her mother had just seen fit to remind her of Bobby.

Jim reached out and petted Esperanza's blazed face. "It's not getting any better on the war front, is it? My son's talking about enlisting. Can't say my wife and I are keen on the idea. But I'd be remiss, Rafe, if I didn't thank you for your service. I'm sorry you paid such a high price."

Rafe shrugged offhandedly, but Alexa knew he must feel like a fraud when it was his buddies who had made the greater sacrifice.

Jim Buckley filled Alexa in on a little local gossip then finally said, "I'd best be getting along home. According to my mobile radio, another storm is moving into the area. Call me if you can't deliver the mare tomorrow."

Alexa scanned the sky. Clouds were building, the kind that tended to bring afternoon or evening thunderstorms. "I couldn't disappoint a girl on her twelfth birthday, Jim. I'll plan on hitting your ranch around noontime tomorrow."

They shook on it and Alexa walked with Jim to his Hummer.

As she watched he vehicle travel down her lane, she realized Rafe had gone in. It was probably difficult for him to see Esperanza sold. Training the mare had been Rafe's first step toward self-reliance.

Realistically, the sale would give her funds for the winter. Locating a buyer for Tano would be icing on the cake and ensure she'd have money to purchase other horses to train next spring. Had Rafe been serious about becoming a business partner? He was a complex man and ran hot, then cold on a lot of things. His cutting words this morning had hurt her. Try as she might, she had no idea what had brought them on. The pathetic part was, her feelings for him hadn't changed. And because of that, she didn't feel strong enough yet to confront him and demand some answers.

She spent the rest of the day outside doing tedious chores. With each hour that passed, the sky grew more menacing. She hosed out the smaller of her two horse trailers and when she finished that Alexa cruised through the nightly feeding of her menagerie. The first splatter of a cold rain caught her halfway to the house. In seconds a cloud opened and drenched her. Shaking off chilly raindrops, she decided to have a hot shower before fixing supper, and the whole time she thought of Rafe.

It was time he told her what was eating him.

His bedroom door was partially open, reminding her of the first day she'd looked in on him. Now as then, Rafe lay on his bed, although this time he was fully dressed. As had become his habit, Compadre stretched out on the floor near the bed.

"Rafe, can we talk?"

He sat up, looking wary.

She decided to make an indirect approach. "I'm sorry you had to deal with my mother. It's not that I don't love her. I do. But she can't seem to let go of the incident involving Bobby."

"Is that why you didn't tell her about me? You're afraid she might come down here on her broom if she finds out you've taken on a mixed-race, half crippled ex-soldier, the son of dirt-poor farmers. She'll grant Bobby saint-hood after she sees me."

"What a horrid thing to say. Unlike you, Rafe, I don't use people. I came here with an olive branch. If I inadvertently did something last night to put you in such a foul mood, I'd like to know what. I thought we were pretty darned perfect together." Her eyes shimmered, but she didn't need to wipe away her tears in front of Rafe.

"You *were* perfect last night. Let it go at that."

Alexa planted her hands on her hips. "If that's not a big fat cop-out I don't know what is. If you somehow got the idea I want more from you than you're willing to give, then I apologize."

"Can we save this conversation for another day?"

"No problem. I'll be away tomorrow delivering Esperanza to the Buckley ranch. Stew all day if you'd like." Turning, she stomped out.

Alexa ate a solitary meal and felt more alone than ever. Her cell showed two missed calls, both from her mother. Frankly, she didn't have the desire or the energy to explain or defend

Rafe. For all she tried to defend Bobby, her mother had never changed her opinion.

Alone in her bed later on, Alexa listened to the rain on the roof. She chewed over Rafe's snarky accusation, then worried about delivering the horse if the rain didn't let up. Sometime after midnight, she got up and fixed a cup of tea brewed from California poppy and passionflower with a dash of dried lavender. Over the last few years she'd relied on it to combat insomnia, and in less than an hour she fell asleep.

THE NEXT MORNING, ALEXA felt refreshed. The storm hadn't abated and the night's downpour had washed a fairly wide groove in the ground in front of the horse trailer she had to hook up to her pickup. She backed up, but wasn't close enough to connect the hitch. Afraid of getting her pickup stuck, she tried muscling the trailer forward across the ditch. Its two wheels sank into the mud with a solid *whump*. Alexa wasn't one to swear, but her thoughts turned the air blue.

Compadre loped up and licked her mud-spattered face as she knelt down to study the situation. She heard Rafe call out to her.

"I'm here, trying unsuccessfully to hitch up the horse trailer." She stood and let the sound of her voice direct him. She wasn't planning to ask him for help, but now that he'd come out, she wouldn't refuse his muscle. "It rained so hard last night, it washed a gully between the pickup and the horse trailer. The pickup has no traction, and when I tried to move the trailer over, it got stuck. I hate to ask, but maybe together we can work it free. If you grab the tongue and shove it close to the hitch, I can connect it."

"Sure. But should you even go in this weather?"

"I promised. I can't disappoint a child on her birthday, Rafe."

"Show me how to lift or pull, or whatever."

Alexa placed his hands on the slick tongue. "Lift and move it forward, please. It's almost lined up. Once you set the tongue, I'll anchor it with the pin, hook the chain, and let the pickup do the hard work of pulling it out of the mud. Then I'll be on level ground and can pull out the ramp and load Esperanza."

Twice Rafe's hands slipped off the metal and the tongue fell short of the hitch. "Damn it to hell and back. I can't see where you want me to connect it, Alexa. You need someone else to help you."

"You're really close, Rafe. Can we try again? I'll guide the tongue. Look! We got it!" Bounding up, she hugged Rafe. "After I drive forward, I'll come back and connect the lights. If it's not a huge imposition, could you bring Esperanza out? Last time I delivered a horse up river to Presidio it took half a day so I want to get started. It's a winding, dippy road."

"I'd like to ride along," Rafe said.

Alexa didn't jump at his offer. "Well, I don't mind having company to break up the monotony. But, are you going to be okay letting go of Esperanza, Rafe?"

"I'm good. Buying, training and selling horses is a business. I did offer to put money in your operation, you know."

"Yes, and you've been in a snit ever since," she muttered.

Rafe's grunt was noncommittal. "I'll get the mare. Anything else you want from the barn?"

"A dry pair of gloves from the glove bin. You may want a pair, too. Oh, and grab two slickers off the pegs inside the door. When I delivered Jim's son's horse, I hit a rock in the road and had to change a flat tire. Not that the odds are great of that happening twice, but I like being prepared."

It didn't take long to load up. Alexa chose a well-maintained fire road that angled through the park. "I'm grateful to the park rangers for tending this road. It cuts twenty miles off the trip. Otherwise I'd be forced to drive into Lajitas to connect with El Camino del Rio."

"I've never been as far north as Presidio. We call the southern section plain old River Road. Isn't the northern part more isolated?"

"Yes, but it's a pretty drive." She glanced guiltily over the top of Compadre's head. "I'm sorry you can't enjoy the scenery, Rafe."

"With the window open for Dog, I can smell the river and get whiffs of wet trees."

"This highway traces the Rio Grande in a series of climbs, dips and twists. I say that so you won't fret. On a good day, and without pulling a lopsided horse trailer, this drive is like a carnival ride."

"Why is the trailer lopsided?"

"It's made to carry two horses. I tried to fasten Esperanza in the center. But I can feel every time she shifts her weight to one side or the other." There were other pitfalls Alexa didn't mention to Rafe. Her pickup was old, and in one area known as The Hill, a mile-high upgrade was sure to tax her truck's aged engine. And on her last trip to Presidio she'd almost hit a cow, because once over The Hill, much of the land near Buckley's ranch was open range.

If she'd hoped Rafe would be chatty, that was a mistake. He took up a third of the bench seat, and remained silent as a rock.

The tension finally got to Alexa. "Rafe, since we're going to be in this cab for long miles, why not get what's bugging you off your chest?"

"Nothing is." He continued to pet Compadre, and turned away from Alexa.

The collie's eyes were closed. His swishing tail whipped across Alexa's leg.

"Like heck," she shot back. Still, Rafe didn't unburden his soul.

Soon, Alexa had more to worry about than Rafe's moody silence. Instead of the storm moving off, the clouds grew blacker. Rain gusted, forcing her to up the speed on the windshield wipers, and she could hear Esperanza growing more restless.

Up ahead she could see the muddy waters of a swollen Rio Grande slapping against its bank. The only plus this time of year—there was zero traffic.

"We've come to the limestone cliffs on your side of the road, Rafe," Alexa said, hoping to take her mind off the worsening conditions. "Until we get to Presidio, this country is desolate except for an occasional adobe home perched on top of those cliffs. This land probably looks the same as it did to the first settlers. I hear those places on the cliffs are mostly summer homes. I envy the owners. They must be able to see all the way across the river into Mexico." She sighed. "There's something about flowing water that I love."

Rafe's shoulders relaxed. "Me, too. Or I did when I could see. When I was eleven or so, Mike, Joey and I used to float down the Terlingua river on inner tubes. All the way to where it intersected the Rio Grande. If our moms had found out, they'd have whipped our butts." He smiled crookedly, and it amazed Alexa how that one smile could melt her irritation.

"Boys get to have all the fun. My mother would have freaked." Her pickup engine choked as she geared down to start the climb up The Hill. Alexa held her breath until the front wheels of the pickup topped the ridge. Then she released a long, heavy sigh.

Rafe stretched his left arm over Compadre and touched her shoulder. "What's the matter? Is the engine running rough? That was the mother of all sighs."

Considering he brushed off her questions about what was bothering him, he had some nerve thinking he had a right to ask her the same question. She glossed over her concerns. "It's raining harder and the driving's more challenging. Luckily, we're over the worst part of the road."

Rafe seemed to accept that explanation. "How close are we to Buckley's ranch?" he asked.

"We're just passing through Presidio. His ranch is another ten miles or so."

Finally they arrived at their destination, and Rafe climbed out to help unload the birthday horse. Wind almost ripped the door from his grasp.

Ordinarily Compadre would have mowed

Rafe down to beat him out of the pickup, curious as to what was going on. Not today. He paced on the seat from one side of the cab to the other, then with a whimper, hunkered down on the floor.

"What's wrong with Dog?"

Alexa pulled out the ramp and unlatched the back door of the horse trailer. "He doesn't like rain. I'm sure it has to do with what happened to him the day I found him half drowned in another bad storm."

Jim Buckley, his wife and two children braved the rain to watch the unloading. "I expected you to call, Alexa, and cancel," Jim shouted. "Alexa, Rafe, this is my wife, Heather, my son, Parker, and Devon, the birthday girl."

"I wouldn't disappoint a birthday girl," Alexa said. "Esperanza's a great horse. You're one lucky kid."

"I know. And I love her name, too." Devon bounced around excitedly on her toes, one hand protecting her eyes from the driving rain. "Daddy, Mama, she's beautiful," the girl said as Rafe backed the mare down the ramp. "Oh, I can't wait to ride her."

"Honey, you have to wait until the weather

clears," Heather Buckley cautioned. "Right now, we need to get her into her stall."

Alexa let Rafe go with the horse. She donned a slicker and closed up the trailer before she, too dashed out of the slanting rain into the barn.

Jim Buckley bent to accept his daughter's bear hug. "Say," he said, straightening. "We were about to sit down for hot tortilla soup, homemade bread and chocolate birthday cake. Why don't you two join us, get warmed up and dry off before you set out for home again. There's plenty."

"Indeed there is," Heather seconded.

Alexa fumbled for an acceptable way to decline that wouldn't hurt these kind people. To her great surprise, Rafe accepted their invitation.

"Hot soup, bread and cake sounds like it'll hit the spot. What do you say, Alexa?"

She couldn't believe he'd be willing to eat soup with virtual strangers. It had taken him long enough to get comfortable with eating in front of her. She also had real concerns about a storm that showed no sign of abating. But after all, they'd have to stop to eat anyway. "Something hot for the belly sounds fantastic.

First, though, I need to convince my dog to take a turn along your fence. He hates rain."

"I'll get him," Rafe offered. "You go on in out of the weather, Alexa. Is his leash still under the driver's seat?"

"Yes. But, Rafe, you'll get soaked."

"I brought a slicker. Let me do this, Alexa. You have to drive both ways. Walking Dog is little enough."

"Uh, okay, Rafe. Thanks."

Jim Buckley turned up the collar on his jacket. "This day's not fit for man nor beast. Rafe, bring the dog inside afterward. We have a big, lazy mutt. I've never known him to twitch an ear when the kids' friends bring their dogs into the house. If it presents a problem, Parker can put Shad in his room."

Rafe loped off to the pickup after acknowledging Jim.

Alexa followed the family, but kept turning to watch Rafe.

Did he think she took charge too often? Had he felt the same way about their lovemaking?

On the drive home she wasn't going to let him off the hook. She didn't care if she made Rafe uncomfortable. She'd fallen for him, and wanted to see where those feelings would take them. They had miles to travel, and they would iron things out, or it wouldn't be for her lack of trying.

CHAPTER ELEVEN

DEVON WAS EAGER TO TALK about her barrel-racing plans during lunch. Alexa was surprised Rafe entered the conversation. But he knew some of the top women barrel racers and spoke animatedly with Devon until her mother emerged from the kitchen holding a cake with twelve flaming candles.

They all chimed in to sing "Happy Birthday."

"Blow out the candles, princess," Jim said, tugging on Devon's braid. She tried, but all they did was blink and sparkle again.

"Parker, you bought trick candles, didn't you?" Devon accused when her older brother convulsed with laughter.

"I couldn't resist, squirt. Here, I'll put them out and pull them off. Dad got a good picture of your shocked expression."

"Honestly," Heather said, turning to

their guests. "I apologize for our children's antics."

Rafe laughed heartily. "Puts me in mind of things my sister used to pull on me. Making memories that carry you through life is what family is all about," he mused, looking relaxed and content. Unexpectedly, he slid a hand under the table and lightly squeezed Alexa's knee.

"Who wants chocolate cake?" Heather said when Parker came back to the table after disposing of the trick candles. No one declined, and Jim cut generous slices while Parker dipped out ice cream. Other gifts were brought out and piled in front of Devon. Once the kids went off to try a new interactive Xbox game Devon got and her brother coveted, Jim handed Alexa a check, completing the sale of the mare.

Pocketing the money, Alexa rose. "Lunch was an unexpected treat, but since it hasn't stopped raining, we need to head out, I'm afraid. Thanks so much to both of you."

"Yes," Rafe added. "You have a great family, Jim."

Their hosts walked Rafe and Alexa to the door, where they collected Compadre. Before they stepped outside, Jim murmured, "In the barn, before we came in for lunch, I heard Parker asking questions about the army, Rafe. Thanks for that slice of honesty. We'd rather he start with college. He's so young. Only seventeen."

"There's good and bad that comes with a career in the military," Rafe replied. "As a bronc riding champion I was still a self-centered kid. The army made a man out of me."

Alexa glanced obliquely at Rafe. That was one of the few positive things she'd heard him say about his army experience.

They parted from the Buckleys and Rafe carried Compadre to the pickup, because the dog fussed about setting foot outside.

Once they were buckled in and under way, Rafe said almost exactly what she was thinking.

"They're nice people. Their house has the feel…the smell of a home."

"What's a home supposed to smell like?"

"Like the Buckleys'. Like Sierra's. And yours. Haven't I told you what I like so much about your place? All war zones reek of motor oil, spent explosives and sweat. And the hospitals smell of antiseptic and blood. Your spicy teas and flowery lotions helped me not think of the stench of war. I owe you more than I can say for that, Alexa."

"Really? I recall the day after you arrived on my doorstep, you hated my tea and accused me of trying to poison you."

"I was a jerk," he mumbled, raking a hand through the dog's fur. "Spending the last hour or so with the Buckleys drove home what I've missed by being a career soldier. No home, no wife, no kids."

Alexa could tell that came from his heart, and she softened a bit toward him. "Don't say that like your life's over, Rafe. You happen to be talking to a woman who knows you're a man in his prime," she added wryly.

"Right," he snorted. "I know I'm no great catch in my present condition, Alexa. A condition that's likely permanent, according to VA docs. I wish I'd told you this before—you gave me a reason to want to live again. Shoot, I know my timing stinks, but I…I…love you, Alexa."

Stunned by his confession, Alexa blindly struck back. "I find that hard to believe. Let me tell you, buster, these past two days you've had a damn funny way of showing it! Love shouldn't hurt."

"What do you mean, Alexa!" His voice was rough enough to bring Compadre up to his feet with a sharp bark. "You're the one who's been hiding out in the barn since we made love. Well, I know I was inept in bed. I can't even open a damned condom. I make more work for you around the house. Today, hooking up a simple trailer, I blew it. You have every right to be mad. I have nothing to offer a woman as capable, as smart and all-together as you are, Alexa. But I needed to say what I feel—like it or not."

"Rafe, I can't process this sudden about-face of yours. Surely you don't think I want to make you feel inadequate?"

"No, I do that fine enough on my own. I don't expect you to love me back, either. I know it'd be a crap future to foist on you."

Alexa opened her mouth to object but the pickup was slammed by a wicked crosswind, and a bolt of lightning speared the road in front of them, flashing first on one side of the road, then on the other.

Alexa reared back in her seat. Compadre howled.

"Whoa, take it easy," Rafe murmured. "If that was lightning, it was darned close."

"This storm has turned ugly." Alexa adjusted her grip on the steering wheel. They were approaching The Hill, and the pickup was being buffeted from all sides. Water ran toward her down the steep incline. Clouds hung so low on the horizon, it looked like night instead of midday. The wind and several inches of running water on the road made it difficult to hold the pickup on course. Easing a hand off the wheel, Alexa snapped on the radio. She spun the dial, and picked up a news station from Mexico. She knew a smattering of Spanish, enough to piece together what the newscaster was saying about the Rio Grande flooding.

"Isn't this highway almost level with the river in spots?" Rafe asked. "If I translated that correctly, the announcer is advising people who live near the river to evacuate to higher ground. Should we turn back?"

"There's nowhere to turn around. This spot is called The Hill. We're almost at the top. Maybe going down the other side we'll be better protected from the wind. Rafe, will you straighten Compadre's harness? His fidgeting is distracting."

"Sure." Rafe felt around the quivering animal. "Somehow he's got himself unhooked."

Alexa crested the hill and realized at once she was descending too fast. She pressed on the brake and the empty horse trailer whipped from side to side. Then it fishtailed like a snake. When she overcorrected, the entire trailer flipped on its side. Braking didn't slow her momentum and water on the road sent her into a slide. She didn't panic until she saw they were aimed straight for the river. In front of her where the road should level out, there was nothing but swirling dark water. "Oh no, oh no. God no," she chanted, seeing they had little time to prepare. "Rafe, brace yourself and hang on to Compadre. Unbuckle your seat belt." She heard his snap, but had no time to undo her own.

Almost standing on the brakes, she made a last vain attempt to stop short of the rising river. The trailer struck the back of the pickup and threw them sideways. Alexa's head hit the driver's window hard. She felt fleeting pain before her air bag exploded, knocking the breath out of her. Gasping, she looked ahead to see a bolt of lightning hit the outside antenna, enter the cab through the radio, and pop and sizzle across the metal dashboard. Just like July 4th fireworks, was her last coherent thought.

DOG LEAPED INTO Rafe's lap, lurching around in a frenzy. The pickup canted to the left. Rafe didn't know what had happened. He felt the collie's back paws digging into his thigh and knew the vehicle seemed suspended on its side. Dog whirled around and Rafe heard him frantically pawing at Alexa.

A sixth sense, one Rafe had counted on often in battle, sounded a warning. "Alexa?" he shouted, leaning around the dog. He set a hand on the dash and yelped in pain at the hot metal.

Alexa didn't answer. Rafe's heart contracted and his insides went cold. Something was bad wrong. Then his mind switched to autopilot as years of military training kicked in. He had to act quickly.

The dog had gone nuts since Alexa wasn't moving. Rafe realized water was seeping into his boots. Cold water. "Quiet," he bellowed

at the dog. Surprisingly the collie whimpered
and slunk back onto Rafe's lap. Waving an
arm toward Alexa, Rafe encountered a spongy
balloon—an inflated air bag. If there was one
on his side in this old pickup, it remained
intact.

Fear crashed down around Rafe.

Sweat ran in his eyes, and trickled down his
chest. Groping wildly, he found Alexa, and
could tell she was out, but breathing. Intuition
sent shivers crawling up his spine. Whatever
their predicament, he had no time to lose. Not
only was the dog in full panic mode, but water
was now soaking Rafe's knees and climbing
higher.

There was no time to get his bearings. Rafe
ran a hand frantically down the back of the
seat until he located the clasp on Alexa's seat
belt. He stabbed it three times before he felt
the catch release, and as it did, the pickup
tilted farther left.

Jaw clenched, he moved Dog aside and
kicked the front windshield. The boots
Alexa had bought him were filled with water,
weighing him down. Holding his breath, Rafe
shucked his boots, and in the next motion,

shoved the objecting dog out through the opening into the cold water.

He felt down Alexa's inert body, anchored his left hand through her leather belt and pushed her out the opening, thrusting her up, hopefully into fresh air. He attempted to follow, but his shoulders wouldn't fit through. Anxiety clawed at lungs that felt close to bursting. Rafe's greatest fear was that he'd have to let go of Alexa. His entire energy coalesced, and in a last-ditch effort, he broke free of the rapidly filling cab.

Behind him, the pickup began to tumble like a bathtub toy. Rafe surfaced in a river gone mad, and for an insane minute he feared he and Alexa were going to be sucked under.

Rain hammered his head as he treaded water in an effort to stay afloat and keep Alexa's head above water. For a terrible moment he realized he had no earthly idea which direction to swim. His newly professed love for the woman in his arms, and a deeply rooted fear of losing her before they could sort out their differences, had him looking to heaven and filling his mind with an old cowboy motto that had given him strength before. *Being a good cowboy isn't something*

*seen in a rodeo arena, or on a TV screen. It's
something that grows from within a man.*

The cobwebs cleared from his brain. He
knew which way the river flowed. He knew
the wind had been blowing east toward the
mountains—toward land. Slowing his frantic
treading, Rafe listened intently to the wind.
What he heard was the faint sound of a dog
barking. A burst of joy gave him the energy to
fight the river's pull. Kicking hard, scooping
water with his right hand, he shoved at debris
and paddled steadily toward the sound. Too
many times his head dipped below the surface, but he coughed and lifted Alexa higher
with an arm that felt dead.

What if he was swimming in the wrong
direction? Almost too tuckered to continue to
fight, Rafe caught the scent of wet dog, and
wetter earth, and his arms and feet tangled in
weeds. He'd reached land. *Thank God!*

Every muscle in his legs shook as he
dragged his exhausted body and a still limp
Alexa ashore. His taxed lungs hauled in big
gulps of air. The dog sounded closer now,
but thunder still rumbled overhead, making
it hard to tell.

They weren't out of the woods yet. On his

knees, he coughed up water, then he bent Alexa over his arm and pounded her back until the water rushed from her lungs. She went into spasms of coughing, but Rafe was just grateful to know she was alive.

Everything moved in slow motion then. His legs cramped. Both arms felt too heavy to lift. Rafe wanted to lie back and do nothing, but out of nowhere, Dog bounded up. He was shivering and his coat was soaking wet, but he licked their faces then lowered his head and whined. The dog grabbed Rafe's jacket sleeve and tugged until Rafe heard the thin material rip. "Hey, what are you doing?"

A faintly fuzzy white flash hit the earth a short distance away and Rafe knew it was lightning.

He shook Alexa until she raised a hand to stop him. "We can't stay out here in the open. Where do you hurt? You were out cold for a while." Rafe struggled to stand.

Alexa rubbed her head. "I think I hit my head on the window right before the air bag smacked me in the face. I...I feel a knot on the left side of my head." She tried getting up, but fell back. "I'm weak as a kitten. Rafe... how did we get here? I can barely make out the pickup and trailer. The truck's bobbing in the river. The trailer may be caught on a jutting rock. Rafe, you saved us," she said, her voice full of wonderment.

Water swirled around Rafe's ankles. He understood the river was still rising. "I was able to get us out of the pickup, but it was your barking friend here who led me to the bank. I think he's trying to get us to follow him. It'll be evening soon, right? We need to find shelter."

Alexa looped her arms around the dog's neck. "It was weather about this bad when I found him almost drowned in a ditch. Poor doggie. He was worn out from trying to climb out. The sides were so muddy, he kept sliding back down." Alexa's voice sounded hoarse. She tried again to stand, but sank to her knees. "You go find a place, Rafe. I don't have the energy. I…I can't seem to catch my breath."

"You probably inhaled too much water." Reaching down, Rafe took her arm and slung her up over his back in a fireman's carry. "We're all going to find shelter. Go, boy," he instructed the dog. "I'll do my best to follow."

Rafe's socks were no cushion against sharp

rocks and downed limbs. During lightning strikes he saw enough smudgy outlines to aim uphill for what he hoped was a stand of trees. Unsure how long he slogged up the slick, rocky incline, Rafe was beyond relieved when the collie barked just ahead of him. Walking over, he realized the dog stood under a canopy of what smelled to Rafe like wet pine mixed with fragrant cedar. Best of all, the ground felt dryer.

Gently, he set Alexa down, then propped his back against a substantial tree trunk. He slid down until his tired butt hit the ground.

"RAFE?" ALEXA LEVERED herself up and pressed her free hand to her still throbbing head. "I…did I black out again?"

Rafe crawled over to her and began sliding his hands up her legs and over her arms, checking for other injuries. When he got to her head, he touched a goose-egg-sized lump, and she shied away, moaning, "Oooh, oooh."

"You have a knot the size of my fist, but I don't feel any blood."

Alexa felt under his fingers. "It hurts like fury, but I don't think it's split. Luckily I have a hard head." She tried to laugh, but stopped, because it hurt too much. "I'm scraped and bruised, but alive thanks to you." She kissed Rafe, then hugged Compadre, who sat panting close beside her. Then she started to cry. "It's my fault we're in this mess. I saw the river had washed over the road or washed it out and I panicked and hit the brakes too hard. Oh, Rafe, I could have killed us all."

"You didn't. It took all of us together to make it this far."

"Don't get all humble. You're my hero, Rafe. Accept that, darn it."

"Okay," he said gruffly. "But hypothermia is our next threat. Where the devil do you suppose we are? And do we have a way of contacting park rangers, border patrol…" Rafe hit the ground with his hand. "Last time I felt such a total lack of control was my last day in Afghanistan."

Alexa dug in her jacket pocket beneath her raincoat. "Oh no, my cell phone is soaked. It won't turn on. Look at you, Rafe. Good grief, your boots are gone, and you have nothing covering your shoulders but a cotton shirt." Swaying woozily, she stripped off her own jacket and tried to drape it over Rafe's shoulders. The sheepskin lining would help warm him.

"Cover Compadre," he said.

She did as he requested, and the dog huddled under the jacket with a grateful woof. "Rafe, that's the first time you didn't call him Dog."

"Yeah, well, if it weren't for him guiding me from the shore, it'd be curtains for you and me. I figure he deserves being called friend in any language."

"You two work well together. When we get out of here, I'm going to cook you both a steak. Then you and I have some other unfinished business," she said, stretching up to kiss the underside of Rafe's jaw.

He passed a hand over the spot, and his lips quirked up in a smile Alexa saw thanks to another burst of lightning, although farther away this time.

"Less rain is making it down through the branches," Rafe muttered. "I guess the storm is moving away. Damn, but I feel so blasted useless."

"I won't listen to that kind of talk, Rafe. After what you just did, you shouldn't ever feel useless again. And don't say Compadre got us out of the pickup, because I know that would be impossible."

"During training for swamp fighting, I learned there's a weak spot in the rubber grommet that holds in a windshield. If you kick it with enough force, it pops right out. The heels on the boots you bought me came in handy, Alexa. But I couldn't swim in them. Sorry I had to ditch them."

"I'll buy you another pair. Two. Even if I hadn't been knocked out, I probably would've drowned. I know park rangers say if you hold your breath and roll down a side window after your submerged vehicle settles, there's time to get out. But I was already feeling panicky. You were the one who stayed calm and collected."

"Quit with the pats on the back, already," Rafe protested. "We're not out of danger yet. I hate to have to hike back down to the road. It's too dark for you to see if the river's risen over the highway."

"We are in a pickle, aren't we, Rafe? We're not expected anywhere. The Buckleys have no reason to think we didn't make it home. We're really stuck. Oh, Rafe, we could die out here." She started to cry again. "Whatever happens, Rafe, I want you to know I love you exactly the way you are." Alexa was close to hysterical, but the floodgates had opened.

Rafe wrapped her in his arms. "Just hold that thought, okay? Listen, you're hurt and frazzled now. We both had our say before we went into the Rio Grande. I promise you, sweetheart, we aren't going to die out here. We only need to formulate a plan."

Alexa took comfort from his words and his arms. "I trust you, Rafe."

"Good." He let a few minutes pass. "When we were driving to Buckley's, you mentioned adobe homes above the road. I know you said they're summer places, and it's well past summer. But if you step out from under the trees, I wonder if you can see lights in any of them. If not, our only choice is to pick our way back down to the road and hike up The Hill to Presidio even if it takes all night."

"That hill alone presents a tough climb, Rafe, and we already know the road might be flooded. But I'll go have a look. Compadre, stay with Rafe," she commanded, because the collie got up when she got did.

Alexa trudged off. She wasn't gone long. "There is one house lit," she said excitedly.

"We must have floated downriver farther than I thought. The homes on the ridge are still west of this stand of trees. My watch has stopped, but, Rafe, it must be six or seven o'clock. Should we wait here until morning? I mean, who knows what we may run into out there in the dark."

"Trouble is, we can't be sure we won't get hit by a second storm. The radio station you turned on suggested more rain on the way. My gut instinct says to hit civilization as quickly as possible. Hopefully get to a place where there's a phone. I can call Doug. He'll know who to contact to rescue us, Alexa."

"You're right. I expected to be back home tonight. I have animals needing to be fed. I really screwed up. I should have listened when you asked if it would be better to delay delivering Esperanza."

Rafe hugged her. "No regrets, Alexa. Be thankful we got out alive. Be thankful it happened on our way home, after we delivered Esperanza. Of course, your pickup and trailer are goners."

"Things, Rafe. It was my grandfather's pickup and trailer. Both saw a lot of use in their day. I learned a long time ago that things aren't anywhere near as important as people." She hooked her arms around his neck and pulled his head down to where she could press damp, teary kisses over his face.

"Enough," Rafe said, brushing the tip of her nose. "Time we got going."

Compadre, who sensed something was up, rose and shook off Alexa's jacket. She bent and scrubbed him as dry as she could.

"How's your head now?" Rafe asked.

"Tender, but at least I'm not dizzy."

Travel was rough. Being a natural leader, Rafe wanted to break trail behind the dog. The second time he bruised his shins on a fallen log and caused Alexa to crash into his back, she grabbed his arm.

"I know cowboys and soldiers expect to be trailblazers, but I'm the eyes for our ragtag group. I can't bring up the rear and be anyone's eyes."

Rafe whistled to Compadre, who continued to crash ahead through the underbrush. For all the energy they'd expended, they really hadn't gone far.

"I should be able to protect you, but can't," Rafe grumbled.

"Funny, I always thought a partnership

meant working together. Weighing each person's strengths and weaknesses, then utilizing the best in both. From my perspective here, maybe because I still have my boots on, it seems I'm the better candidate to lead. At this rate your feet will be cut to ribbons before we're halfway to our destination." Alexa couldn't believe they were standing here arguing, freezing cold, exhausted and basically lost. Stubborn man. "Can't it be enough for your ego to know you got us this far?"

"Put that way, Alexa, I suppose it can. But if—when—we make it back to your ranch, you'd better look back on this and start believing in yourself as the capable woman I know you are."

"What are you talking about?"

"I'll agree to quit brooding over the loss of my eyesight if you cut yourself slack and stop taking the blame for Bobby Duval's death. You've let your mother hold it over your head too long."

Alexa expelled a sudden, deflating breath. "How did you guess?" she said.

"Because I was guilty of the same thing. After Mike and Joey were killed, I thought

I'd lost the ability to save anyone, including myself. Today, I learned different."

Alexa didn't speak. She simply wove her arms around Rafe's waist and lifted her face up to his for a long, satisfying kiss. They clung together, savoring and accepting the truth of Rafe's words until Compadre's insistent barking pulled them apart.

"We'd better see what he's found," Rafe finally said, slowly releasing Alexa.

What next, she thought.

Hand in hand, they picked their way uphill, following the dog. The prize he wanted to show them proved to be a trail of sorts that zigzagged up to a dozen or so steps carved out of the limestone cliff. Steps that led up to the top of the ridge to a level, graveled area between two adobe homes.

"We made it! We made it!" Alexa hopped up and down with joy. "I'm tempted to get down on my knees and kiss the ground right here," she told Rafe.

"Who's out there?" a man shouted through the darkness. "I have a rifle. If this is your dog, come get him, and identify yourselves."

"Don't shoot, don't shoot," Alexa and Rafe shouted in unison. Alexa grabbed Rafe's hand

and tried to run along a gravel path in the direction of Compadre's barking. Rafe hobbled behind her on obviously tender feet.

"I delivered a horse to Jim Buckley, up past Presidio, around noon today," Alexa called out. "We got caught in the worst of the storm. At the bottom of The Hill, our pickup and trailer hit a washout and plunged us into the river. Rafe got us out." She turned back and held tight to his arm.

"Here, I'll let go of your dog and snap on the porch light," a man's voice said. "I can see you're bedraggled all right. My name is Pete Johnston. My wife thought she saw a pickup floating in the river. Come on in. God only knows how you made it out of that river, let alone climbed up here."

"I went through worse in Afghanistan," Rafe said, "and I'd appreciate if you'd uncock that rifle. We don't mean you any harm. In fact, I'll give you the phone number of my brother-in-law. He's a border patrol agent. Doug Martinez is his name."

Alexa gazed up at Rafe. She'd had no idea the man on the porch hadn't engaged the catch on his weapon. She squeezed Rafe's arm.

"I'm Laurie Johnston," a woman said,

stepping out of the home. "Pete, put down that gun. It's not even loaded." She sounded exasperated. "I told you I saw a truck down in the river. Let these poor people and their dog come in and warm up. Can't you see they're soaked and too out of breath to be a threat to a flea?"

"Well, with our neighbors gone, we can't be too careful," her husband grumbled.

"We're grateful for your hospitality." Alexa took Rafe's hand, and hooked his other through Compadre's collar. She began to tell their story to Laurie Johnston as she escorted them into a wood-beamed living room, and brought towels for them to dry themselves with in front of the toasty fire.

Laurie served hot chocolate and roast beef sandwiches, but before Alexa could finish hers, she had drifted off to sleep.

DOUG MARTINEZ DETERMINED that there was room to land a border patrol helicopter in the keyhole turnaround at the end of Pete Johnson's gravel road. He promised to dispatch someone right away.

Even then it was well after midnight before

Doug's friend, a chopper pilot, delivered the three weary travelers back to Alexa's ranch.

On landing, Alexa discovered their ordeal wasn't over. A dark late-model Mercedes was parked beside her porch. At the sound of the helicopter rotors, her parents rushed out of the house. "What are you doing here?" she yelled at them.

"Your mother said she told you we were coming," her father shouted.

"Alexa," her mother exclaimed, "where on earth have you been?"

Rafe, who had stopped to thank the pilot, apparently heard the outburst. He stepped up behind Alexa and put his hands on her shoulders. "Mr. and Mrs. Robinson. Alexa's had a rotten day. She could use a hot shower and a night's sleep. I'll be glad to fill you in on why she got home late. We lost her pickup and empty horse trailer in the Rio Grande. The three of us were lucky to swim ashore. I phoned my brother-in-law when we got to a phone and he arranged transport home in that helicopter." Rafe waved in the vicinity where the whirlybird now lifted off.

Alexa reached back and took his hand. "Rafe's right. Let's all go inside."

Her mother sniffed haughtily as Alexa dragged Rafe into the house, but her dad enveloped her in a big hug.

"Daddy," Alexa protested feebly. "I'm grubby, and your suit must be an Armani." But she was glad to feel his arms around her. When she finally pulled back, she said, "Mother, Daddy, meet Rafe Eaglefeather."

"Ah, your patient, the soldier." Jason Robinson let go of Alexa to size up her companion.

"Rafe's a former soldier, an ex-rodeo champion, but he's more than a patient. He's the man I love." Alexa lifted her chin to stare down her mother, who gasped.

"In that case, Alexa," her father said, "it seems our family has a lot more to discuss than you missing Thanksgiving in Houston. I suggest we go to the living room and have a stiff shot of the brandy your mother thinks I don't know she packed in her overnight case." He held the door wider and nudged his wife ahead of him. They continued into the living room, but Alexa hung back with Rafe.

"I'm sorry I put you on the spot just now, Rafe."

"No problem. Shall we just get the grilling over with?"

Alexa sagged against him. "You've no idea how hot the grill can get. When my mother gets started, she's like a rabid alligator."

Rafe laughed, but lowered his voice. "Are there rabid alligators?"

"You'll see. In heels and a designer suit."

He kissed her then. "For you, I'd face a platoon of alligators. You go hop in the shower. I'll put water on for tea. What's calming that goes with brandy?" he asked quietly.

"Wood betony and linden flower. I'll get the jar down. Rafe, did I dream it, or did you say you loved me before we crashed?"

"No dream, and I meant it," he said. "What I didn't get around to asking was...will you marry me, Alexa? I almost lost you today. I never want to go through that again."

She rose on tiptoes and kissed him thoroughly. "Oh, Rafe, I thought you'd never propose. I thought I'd have to ask you and my answer is yes. Yes, I'll marry you. But, wait till I get back to tell my folks, please. Oh, and, Rafe, if you fix Mother's tea...be extra generous with the brandy."

CHAPTER TWELVE

RAFE LISTENED TO THE shower go on. He fed Compadre while waiting for the tea to steep. He was beat. His feet hurt like fury, and his arms felt like they might still fall off. He had told Alexa they should get this meeting with her parents over with, but he wished now they could delay it till morning.

To heck with steeping five minutes. He set the teapot on a tray with cups and carried it into the living room, carefully counting the steps to the small table. He hoped to hell Alexa's parents hadn't moved things around.

"Alexa's showering, so I fixed tea," he said. A fire crackled cheerfully and Rafe wished he could curl up in front of it with Alexa.

Later, he consoled himself, discreetly brushing one knee against the table, to be certain it sat where he remembered.

"What kind of tea?" Alexa's mother asked, sounding petulant.

"A favorite of Alexa's," Rafe said. "Her special blend. Why don't I leave you two to enjoy a cup, while I hit the shower."

"Could you remove this dog?" That request came from Alexa's father. "He's made himself at home in front of the fire, but the heat's left him smelling like a sewer."

Alexa's mother's voice rose over top of her husband's. "Tell me you aren't planning to shower with our daughter."

Rafe held his temper in check. "I'll take Compadre with me to shower in my bathroom. Come," he called, snapping his fingers.

"So, you and Alexa aren't sleeping together? Thank goodness for that," her mother said. "For the life of me I can't understand how a child we raised, Jason, developed this penchant for finding and harboring all manner of strays."

"Kate!" Her husband spoke sharply.

Gritting his teeth, it was all Rafe could do to keep walking down the hall. But could he really blame Alexa's mother? By her own admission, Alexa had taken in Bobby Duval, a James Dean tough-guy. She had a collection of needy animals. And she'd taken him in. If he had a daughter, he probably wouldn't be too happy in similar circumstances.

He hoped he could overcome Kate Robinson's initial opinion of him. After all, Alexa said she loved him. A new believer that love conquered all, Rafe let the steamy spray wash away his anxiety. Anyway, he could only handle one battle at a time. Right now it was soaping and rinsing off a forty-pound collie who hated to be bathed.

Rafe persisted and emerged the victor. The result after he rubbed them both dry with a mountain of towels was that both he and Compadre smelled better.

ALEXA WATCHED RAFE ENTER the living room where she sat stiffly on the couch. She jumped up and ran to take his arm. "Come sit beside me, Rafe. I'll pour your tea, and add a shot of brandy."

Rafe bent down and deliberately kissed Alexa. He heard a strangled hiss from the direction of her mother's chair, but he didn't pull away. He could think of few better ways to start the ball rolling than by staking his claim.

Her father cleared his throat. Half rising

from his chair, he picked up the bottle of brandy and tipped a finger or two in each cup. "Alexa gave us a rundown on your impressive military record, Major."

"What are your plans after you leave Alexa's?" her mother rushed to say. "More therapy at one of the VA Centers?"

Jason set down the bottle and extended the first cup to Rafe.

Alexa took the cup out of her dad's hand and set it back on the table. Tugging Rafe down beside her on the couch, she said, "Your cup is sitting on the right edge of the coffee table. It's a foot reach with your right hand, Rafe."

He squeezed the hand Alexa held, and with the other easily found the cup. "Actually, I'm not planning on leaving. Alexa and I have discussed expanding the business by adding quarter horses to her training program."

Kate picked up her cup. "Of course Jason and I can't thank you enough for pulling Alexa out of that wreck today. That's a horrible bruise she has on her head. And she explained how she hit the side window and it knocked her out. We are grateful...." She fumbled for words, but with a gesture, tossed the ball back to her husband. "Aren't we, Jason? But…"

"Kate, I don't know what you're pussyfooting around trying to say," he snapped.

"Oh, you do, too. You know as well as I do that Alexa's sequestered herself in this no-man's-land long enough. That unfortunate incident with the Duval boy is over and best forgotten. It's high time Alexa comes back to Houston, opens a new holistic practice and gets on with her life."

"Mother, I love it here, and I'm not moving back to Houston."

"Nonsense, dear. What kind of life is it for you out here—feeding and doctoring all these strays."

"Including me," Rafe said deliberately, knowing he was the crux of Mrs. Robinson's objections.

"Stop!" Alexa leapt up. "I will not sit here and listen to you try to rearrange my life again, Mother. Have you forgotten who insisted I move here when the media assassinated my character? You think you can order my life around whenever it suits you. You've never bothered to ask my opinion. You try to organize me like I'm one of your charities. You have since I started school."

"That's not true," her mother said, sounding aghast. "I did spend time with your teachers, but all parents do. And your father and I both did all we could to help you find a suitable, appropriate career when teachers explained what a genius you were."

"Right. You thought if I was a doctor I wouldn't stray outside of Houston's elite circle."

Jason set his cup down with a clatter. "Whatever gave you that notion? Your mother and I are ordinary people. We both came from hardworking stock. We didn't know how to react to having such a bright child. Your teachers were the ones who said you had aptitude in science and should be a doctor."

"We wanted the very best for you," Kate cried. "That wasn't the Duval boy, and if you'd admit it, he proved us right. We know you did nothing to harm him. His parents were greedy through and through. It almost killed us to see the damage he—they—did to your career, and how that sucked the life out of you. So, yes, Alexa, we're upset now. It seems a bit like history is repeating itself."

"You never understood Bobby wasn't like his parents," Alexa said. "He looked up to Dad, and he had dreams. He worked so hard. He did a good job, or you would have fired him, Daddy. What Bobby did for me was make me laugh and show me how to not take life so seriously. He was my only real friend. As for Rafe, he's given me back my self-esteem. We like the same things. Horses. Dogs. Ranching. He asked me to marry him tonight, and...I said yes."

"Oh, Alexa." Her mother rushed over and took her daughter's hands. "Honey, I know right now you feel indebted to Rafe because he saved you today. But consider what it means to be someone's caregiver long-term. I know what it's like to be tied down. My mother was an invalid. I took care of her when I should have been a carefree child."

Her mother was speaking as if Rafe wasn't in the room, but it was useless to try to stop her once she was on a roll. "That has nothing to do with us, Mother. If you think Rafe needs me more than I need him, you're mistaken. And he's far from an invalid." Alexa scooted closer to Rafe to grab his arm. "We're partners. Equal in every way. Please, can't you be happy for us?" She leaned her head on Rafe's shoulder.

He looped an arm around her. "Alexa, you humble me," he said with feeling.

"Well, Kate," her husband said, "it seems congratulations are in order."

"Yes, yes, I suppose they are," Kate agreed, returning to her seat with an air of defeat.

Rafe cleared his throat. "At our age, we don't really need your blessing to get married, Mr. and Mrs. Robinson. But…it'd please me if you could see your way to give it. I lost my parents when I was fourteen. Family is important to me. I want Alexa to keep hers. And our children will need grandparents."

"Oh, Rafe." Alexa fluttered her fingers along his jaw. "I was prepared to set aside my desire to have children for you. I wasn't sure you wanted them. I know you seemed hesitant around your sister's brood."

"I felt uneasy around them because I can't see."

"Rafe, I hope for your sake you regain your sight. But I love you as you are. Frankly, raising children can't be much different from training horses. And you're marvelous at that."

"Alexa, I still can't believe you love me."

"Ahem." Her father cleared his throat. "Kate, I propose we toast the happy couple. It's getting late. We're not as young as Rafe and Alexa. We need our beauty sleep. Gone are the days we stayed up all night necking."

His wife nearly choked, but Jason chuckled and went around topping off their cups with brandy. "Alexa, Rafe, earlier I looked over this property. Tomorrow I want to talk to you both about putting a wind farm on that slope behind the house. You can make enough so that raising horses can be a hobby."

"Jason Robinson, what kind of toast is that?" Kate exclaimed, doing her best to stifle a yawn. She rounded the table and touched Rafe's arm. "I apologize if I sounded rude before. All I've ever wanted, truly, is for Alexa to be happy. I guess maybe I never really knew just what she wanted. But I can see she's happy now, and for that I thank you. Jason and I do give our blessing."

Alexa hugged Rafe before she raised her cup and clinked it with his first, then with her dad's and mother's. Compadre, who'd been snoozing by the fire, lifted his head and gave a little yip when they all loudly said, "Cheers!"

Kate gathered the empties. "I'll wash these, dear. I hope you and Rafe will settle on a wedding date soon. You may as well know, Rafe, I've imagined the kind of wedding Alexa should have from the day I bought her christening gown. Remember, Valentine's Day is beautiful and doable in Houston. Rafe, you'll look handsome in a cutaway tux, or if you'd rather wear your dress uniform…"

"Mother," Alexa threw up her hands. "I thought something small, here at the ranch. The animals…"

"Jason will arrange to fly in a qualified pet-sitter. You'll need someone to stay while you're on your honeymoon. Paris, perhaps?"

"Mother…"

Rafe wrapped his arms around Alexa from behind, bent his head and nipped her ear. "Let your mom do this for you, sweetheart. Let your dad walk you down the aisle. Have the works. I look forward to doing that for any daughters we have."

Alexa turned in Rafe's arms. They were still kissing when her parents hurried off to the kitchen with the tray of empty cups.

Rafe pulled back to whisper in Alexa's ear, "It wasn't too terrible. Even rabid alligators have a soft spot when it comes to love."

Alexa's laugh was muffled by another kiss, one that continued well after her parents retired. It was a love-affirming kiss that said the two of them were ready and eager to embark on a long, happy, passionate and spirited future together.

* * * * *

LARGER-PRINT BOOKS!
GET 2 FREE LARGER-PRINT NOVELS PLUS
2 FREE GIFTS!

HARLEQUIN®

Super Romance®

Exciting, emotional, unexpected!

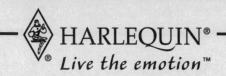

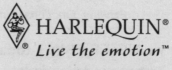

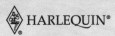

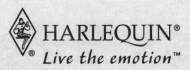

Harlequin® Historical
Historical Romantic Adventure!

Imagine a time of chivalrous knights and unconventional ladies, roguish rakes and impetuous heiresses, rugged cowboys and spirited frontierswomen— these rich and vivid tales will capture your imagination!

Harlequin Historical . . . they're too good to miss!

Silhouette®

SPECIAL EDITION™

Emotional, compelling stories that capture the intensity of living, loving and creating a family in today's world.

Special Edition features bestselling authors such as Susan Mallery, Sherryl Woods, Christine Rimmer, Joan Elliott Pickart— and many more!

For a romantic, complex and emotional read, choose Silhouette Special Edition.

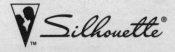

Silhouette®

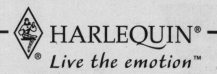